In-Between

A Story of Redemption

Beca Lewis

PERCEPTION PUBLISHING

Contents

The only reason for time is so that everything doesn't happen at once. —Ray Cummings, The Time Professor

Time and space are modes by which we think and not conditions in which we live. —Albert Einstein

The distinction between the past, present and future is only a stubbornly persistent illusion. —Albert Einstein

ONE

No one expected her to die. She wasn't that old. She hadn't been sick.

One night she lay down on her bed and never got up again. Or so they said. Not to her. To each other. No one spoke to her. She tried to speak. But no one heard her. She had finally become invisible, as she had often wished to be.

It had been a beautiful spring day. The daffodils bobbed their glorious yellow heads in the breeze, and the buds on the maple tree branches shone red in the sunlight.

The pussy willow tree at the end of the yard spread open its soft buds against the brilliant blue sky. She had stood under it, admiring its perfection, and watched white clouds drift by, looking as if they were weaving themselves between the branches.

Neighbors up and down the street had come outside. They were checking their lawns to see what winter had done to them, and waving, delighted to see each other on this glorious day. The children were riding their bikes down the middle of the street, confident that no cars would dare bother them.

Spring had come. The days had lengthened, and the temperature no longer dropped below freezing at night. An easy winter had not diminished the joy of the arrival of spring.

While the neighborhood rejoiced in a beautiful day, Connie Matthews had kept her emotions in check. Connie believed that being too happy, or too sad, was a dangerous thing.

For Connie, that day had been good. Not great. But good. Okay. Just as life had been for the past fifty years. She woke up, made her bed, and swept the floor for any crumbs that might have escaped her careful eye the day before.

Although Connie often left food out for the animals that visited her yard, she didn't want a mouse coming into her house searching for food. That was not where they were supposed to be living. They had other places to live. This was her home—hers, not theirs.

Connie hated capturing mice. At first, she had live-trapped them. But there always seemed to be more. It occurred to her that perhaps they were returning to the house. One day she dabbed a drop of red nail polish on a mouse's tail before releasing it.

The day she trapped that same mouse again, she had to admit that they were finding their way back to her home.

Hating it, but knowing it was the only way, she had resorted to using traps that killed them instantly. At least she hoped so. Every time one died in the trap, Connie prayed that they would not come back and haunt her dreams.

In high school botany class, they had been required to capture bugs, kill them, preserve them, and pin them onto boards. After two days of capturing, killing, and pinning, Connie had nightmares of the bugs flying down the tiny hallway to her room and torturing her.

Connie was never sure who had intervened for her. Maybe she did it herself. Perhaps she had spoken up and told the teacher what was happening. She hoped that was what she did—that she had spoken up and did something instead of letting it happen to her.

But whoever spoke to the teacher had somehow persuaded him that there was another way to study bugs. She never had to kill again. Until the mice.

But to Connie, this was different. There was no preserving the mouse and pinning it to a board for further study. That meant it might have a chance. If there was something like life after death, perhaps it ran off to join the other mice in some other place. Maybe a place better than this one.

So as Connie released the dead mice from the trap, she would send it off in her mind to join its friends. No need to be mad at her for doing what she had done. Her house was not made for mice.

The morning she died, Connie had found a mouse in the trap. She had put the body near the tiny stream that ran through the small woods behind her house. She didn't believe that the body was a mouse anymore, and maybe the hawk would enjoy a free meal. Perhaps then it would not bother her birds because it would be full of mouse instead.

Her birds were Connie's pride and joy. If they were in her yard, her woods, her garden, they were her birds. She watched them through the windows of her living room, and the glass door in her bedroom. She had feeders everywhere, and birdhouses, too.

That day, her last day, she sat in the one chair in her living room and watched the bluebirds choose which house they would build a nest in. They were so indecisive. Or at least it appeared that way to Connie.

For the last month, she had watched them try to pick a home. First, they would peek into each house and then flit over to sit on the next. Sometimes they would go inside the house, poking in their heads first, and she would think "finally." But later, they would be house hunting again. Their indecisiveness drove Connie crazy.

"Pick one, for heaven's sake," she would tell them through the window.

While they played around choosing their homes, the house sparrow would take over the birdhouse. For the first few weeks of spring, she would pull the sparrow nests out of the box, telling the bluebirds that she couldn't do this forever.

She loved the bluebirds, but she hated that they didn't stand up for themselves. She wanted them to take what was theirs. She wanted them to fight the house sparrows when they raided their nests.

In her heart, Connie knew she had become more like the bluebirds. She could decide nothing important. She was afraid to stand up for herself. Afraid to take action. She had made herself into this timid woman. There was no one to blame but herself.

So, instead of living the life she had once dreamed about, she worked in the garden. She would wave at the neighbors. But they knew not to come over.

She had nothing to say. She didn't like gossip, and she didn't care what they did with their own lives. And since she had done nothing with hers, she had nothing to share.

I could have done life differently, Connie thought, as she watched the people stare at the woman in the bed. The woman who looked just like her. Now that it was too late, she knew she should have. She shouldn't have let herself be trapped like the mice in her house. Live trapped, but barely living.

One person standing around the bed was crying. A little. She has to, Connie thought, because Karla would worry about what people would say if she didn't feel sorrow at her mother's death.

But Connie knew better. Karla was relieved. Now she never had to worry about taking care of a mother she barely knew.

Whose fault is that? Connie asked herself.

No one needed to tell her it was her own.

Later they would discover why she had died, but only she knew why she had not lived.

TWO

At first, Connie thought being dead wasn't that bad. No one talked to her, so she didn't have to make up something to say. Since she had no desire to hang around and watch people fake how much they missed her, and there was no way she was attending her own sad funeral, she had started walking. For a while, she loved it. She could go anywhere she wanted, and no one saw her.

She visited the library, the coffee shop, sat in the park, and walked to her favorite garden store. It was lovely. Until it wasn't.

It took only a few days to realize that she was utterly alone, and that was not how she thought it was supposed to be when death arrived. Wasn't someone supposed to meet with her and help her go someplace else?

Wasn't there supposed to be a light to walk towards? She had lived a reasonably exemplary life. Except for that one time, she had stayed out of trouble. If there was a heaven, shouldn't she be going there? Eventually?

But there was nothing. Not even another dead person to talk to. It didn't surprise Connie that there was life after death, but the loneliness of it did. How could she be lonely? Wasn't being alone something she had actively sought?

It also surprised her that she missed having conversations. She spent much of her life hiding away from people so they wouldn't bother her. Although the thought that she had kept away from people because she didn't want to hurt them flashed through her mind, she shut it down as quickly as possible. As she always did.

But if she had wanted not to bother people or hurt them, now her wish had come true. Maybe that's why being dead looked like this.

Perhaps this version of heaven was designed for her because it was what she had wanted. But being totally alone was not as pleasant as she thought it would be.

In fact, by the end of the second day of aimless walking, Connie was desperate to find someone, anyone, to speak to. She tried tapping the people she saw on the shoulder, and when that didn't work, she tried bumping into them.

Once in a while, someone would shudder and look around, but that was it. She would wave at them, scream, even try walking through them, which worked—the walking through part, but not getting their attention.

Finally, she gave up on the live people and started looking for others like her. There had to be more people that were dead and still in town the same way she was. Maybe there was a community of dead people who lived somewhere together.

By then, Connie realized that she was willing to be part of a community of people, if only she could find them.

She was also hungry. Or at least she thought she was. There was a strange sensation of emptiness, and she thought food might fill it. But even though she could walk up to the food she saw everywhere, she couldn't touch it.

Eventually, after finding no one to talk to, she decided to think about the problem logically. First, it was apparent she was dead. Yes, she had figured that out right away. Wasn't that hard. Looking at a body lying in a bed that looked just like her made it pretty obvious.

She was grateful that she had been wearing pajamas because she had no desire to walk around with no clothes on, which was how she used to sleep. However, even though she didn't feel hot or cold, and no one could see her, she didn't like it.

Why and how she died wasn't clear. But perhaps that wasn't important. What was important was to find someone who could tell her what was happening to her. Maybe even show her how to change into something more presentable.

Another few days went by, and finding no one, Connie decided to do something different. She went home. No one was there, just as it had been while she was alive.

There was a for-sale sign on the front lawn. Karla had wasted no time getting rid of the house. When she had left it to Karla—who else would it go to—she had half hoped that Karla would come live in it.

But obviously Karla wanted to forget their life together as quickly as possible. Inside the house, the closets were empty, and half the furniture was gone. Karla is staging the home to make it look good, Connie thought.

Even though she had expected Karla not to care, it still hurt. Surprisingly. Although she couldn't feel cold and heat, she could feel hunger and emotions. That didn't seem fair. For the first time, Connie felt a touch of panic. What if this was what eternity would be like for her?

Sitting alone in the house she used to own, Connie thought about her life, hoping that perhaps that would prime the pump somehow and allow her to move on.

Besides, Connie thought, *what else do I have to do? What if this is eternity?*

That thought terrified her, so she let herself drift back to where it had all begun—in the trailer park, stupidly called King's Row.

She thought back to the day she left that place. Over fifty years ago. How impossible that seemed. But now that she was dead, what did time mean anyway?

THREE

Living in a dump like King's Row had not dampened Connie's thoughts of the future. At eighteen, Connie had seen a lifetime of possibilities stretched out before her. She would conquer the world.

First college, then a career doing something important. She didn't know what that would be yet. What she would choose wasn't essential to know. What was important was that she would be free as a bird. A college had accepted her, and she was leaving home. Forever, as far as Connie was concerned.

There would be no returning to the broken-down trailer she had lived in with a father who came home only long enough to see if his one and only daughter had money that he could steal or con from her.

Connie had been earning her own money since the women in the trailer park had decided that she was old enough to watch their kids while they went out. Sometimes the women actually went someplace useful, like shopping. Other times, Connie suspected they just went anywhere that wasn't home.

Husbands existed for some of those women, but were rarely seen. The men said they were busy trying to earn enough money to bring home. But often it was to spend on what they felt they deserved. After all, since they were the money-makers they could do what they wanted with it. In that way, the men acted like the kings of the trailer park.

To pay Connie for babysitting, the women would squirrel away some grocery money, work at jobs their husbands didn't know about, or sell things they made.

Like Connie, they had learned to hide what they earned. They had come up with many creative hiding places. For a long time, a favorite spot was inside an old face cream jar. But once one husband discovered the money, they all knew. *Some kind of male bonding ritual,* Connie thought.

But that didn't stop the women. They found alternative hiding places and inventive ways to make money. They were always trying to stay ahead of everything and everyone that wanted money from them—from bill collectors to the men in their lives.

As Connie got older, they included her in their secrets. By the time she was eighteen, she thought she understood how the world worked. And she was ready to outsmart it.

All her life the women of King's Row were Connie's bedrock and her family. What they did when they left their trailers didn't bother her. She understood that they had to find life somewhere. At least they came back. Unlike her mother. Whoever she was.

Connie had no memory of her, and there were no pictures around the trailer to give her a clue. Connie had learned long before that asking questions of her father only earned her some form of punishment. If she was lucky, it was the silent treatment. That was preferable to other kinds.

When she turned sixteen, the women who had known her mother told Connie that she looked like her. After that, she had often stood in front of the window, trying to see her reflection. She pretended that it wasn't her standing there; it was her mother. What she saw wasn't much. She wouldn't stand out on the street with her dirty blond hair that hung to her waist.

Looking more like her mother was probably why her father had been increasingly evil-tempered. She doubted it was because she was leaving home. She had told him, but he had paid no attention. Maybe he didn't believe her. Or perhaps he was relieved she was going. It was hard to tell what her father felt. If anything.

Maybe he hadn't considered who would keep the trailer reasonably clean, or make food for him. She had only told him her plans that one time. That's all she owed him. Probably didn't even owe him that. Long years of hiding from him had taught her the art of deception. So she thought that telling him once was enough. What she would never tell him was where she was going.

But she was leaving, and her heart felt as if it would thump out of her chest she was so excited. She had been saving money to go for years. First babysitting, and then once she was old enough, she worked any job she could get.

Despite her terrible home life, or maybe because of it, she had studied hard enough to get a decent score on her SAT because college had always been her goal. She figured that if she could get to college, she would make it out of this life, and she would never return.

But no matter how much she worked, she knew she wouldn't have enough for school. It didn't matter. She knew she would go to college, anyway. Even if it meant it took her ten years to get through college—working, and paying her way as she went—she would make it.

But one night, a miracle happened. A miracle delivered by the women of King's Row. A miracle organized by the woman everyone called Mama Woo.

Connie thought she was going to babysit. But when she reached the trailer, they were all waiting for her. All the women of King's Row stood in the tiny space that passed for a living room with tears in their eyes. Connie thought something terrible had happened, and her world had shattered.

These women had treated her like a daughter. They made sure she had clothes to wear. They told her about boys and babies.

She wasn't surprised that they told her to stay away from boys and even men. "You don't want to end up like us," they would say.

Connie had agreed. She didn't. So she had obeyed the women. Most people would have called the women trailer trash, but Connie knew differently. And she loved them as they loved her.

That night, the tears didn't mean the end of the world for her. It was the beginning. The women told her a secret they had been keeping from the day her mother had disappeared.

Not only had they squirreled away money for getting out of the trailer park and paying her babysitting wages, but they had also saved money for her.

Every week, for sixteen years, they had each put a bit of money into an account in her name. And never told her. They waited until they were sure that she would choose to escape the life she had been born into and become someone. They couldn't replace her mother, but they could help give her a future.

The money that they saved was enough for the first year of school if she wanted to go. She did. So for her last few years of high school, she had worked even harder.

She would make Mama Woo and the women proud of her, no matter what it took.

Two years later, and she was ready. Her clothes were packed and waiting for her in Mama Woo's trailer. Another woman was driving her to the college. It wasn't far. But what it looked like and how she would live was like going to another universe. Connie figured that once there, she would figure out how to get around. She would get jobs to make sure she could eat and pay the next year's tuition when it came due.

A life full of possibilities stretched before her. If she did it right, she could come back and help these women who had been her mother. They had told her "no," never come back. Ever. They needed to know she had escaped. They would find her if they needed her.

But she had returned, and instead of bringing help, she had gone to them because she was in trouble.

So many wonderful things had happened to her by then, Connie had almost forgotten where she had come from. Almost.

FOUR

For Connie, going to college had delivered a one-two punch to the gut. Although it was less than a hundred miles from home, it was as if she had moved to another planet.

She thought she would feel free. Instead, she felt exposed. She was a fraud. She didn't belong there. Everyone moved through the classes, the dorm, and the town as if it was second nature. Groups of people walked together, chatting, laughing, wearing clothes that she could never afford. *What had made her think she would fit in?*

And she was homesick. How that was possible shocked her. She had no idea that she would miss the children she had taken care of for years and the women of King's Row with such intensity. How much a part of her life they had become had not occurred to her until she realized she might never see them again since they told her never to come back.

She didn't miss her father. And she hoped she never saw him again. He didn't know where she had gone. She left a note saying goodbye, but nothing else. It had to be a secret so he couldn't find her. If she ever returned home, it would be when she was successful enough to help the women, but never for him.

But her heart yearned for the love and acceptance she had felt when she was with the women and children who had been her family.

It was only for them that she kept going, dragging herself through each day like it was mud. Knowing that they had scrimped and saved so she could leave home and become somebody was her motivation.

The money they saved not only paid the first year's tuition, but also for her dorm room. They hadn't given her the money directly. They sent it to the college.

Only then did Connie fully realize how wise they were. If she had the cash in hand, she would probably have run away. No. Not probably. She would have. As it was, the college was the only roof she had over her head, and she owed the women to try, so she stayed.

It took a few weeks, but she finally found a part-time job at a tiny hamburger place near the middle of town. She got a free meal every day, which helped her budget.

She tried to get people she met at school and the restaurant to call her Constance instead of Connie, but within the first week, someone used the nickname, and she was back to the name she had heard all her life.

By then, she had realized that she couldn't escape where she came from, even if she changed her name. So she gave up on the idea of Constance and settled into making herself as Connie fit into this new life.

The first thing she did was to cut her hair. It was the first time she had ever been in a beauty shop, and the feeling of being pampered both soothed her and made her anxious.

But when she walked out of the shop up the stairs to the sidewalk, her bob bouncing with every step, she knew it had been the best money she had ever spent.

People turned and looked at her, even a few boys. But she remembered what the women told her. No boys, even if they thought they were men, for now. School first.

It took months, but by the time Thanksgiving and chilly weather arrived, she had begun to feel as if she belonged in that simultaneously strange, exciting, and scary place.

Watching the other students, she had adjusted her looks and her speech to fit in better. And that brought her more attention. Some of it good. Having mirrors and makeup helped. And she began to understand that she had life experiences that would serve her no matter where she went—even college.

It was her roommate's invitation to go home with her for Thanksgiving that changed everything.

She and Edith had not gotten along at first. Connie had to admit it had been entirely her fault. Edith had been friendly from the start. When Connie arrived at the dorm, sweaty and exhausted, Edith Warren was sitting on the bed she had chosen, looking as if she hadn't a care in the world.

As Connie struggled through the door with her one suitcase, Edith had unfolded her legs from the yoga pose she had been sitting in and came to help. Her shiny ebony hair swung like a curtain over her face as she bent down to pick up the bag that Connie had set down to open the door.

"I'll get it!" Connie had snapped at her, and Edith had pulled back, startled at Connie's tone of voice. But instead of reacting, Edith started gaily chatting about how happy she was to meet Connie and bombarding her with questions. Where was she from, what was her major, did she want to go out to lunch?

Connie had answered all of Edith's questions with a grunt, or a "no" until Edith had given up and left Connie in the room alone with the realization that she didn't fit in and had no idea what was she going to do about it.

She had smacked her pillow in frustration at being stuck with this bubbly girl who probably was off talking with her friends about the hick from the sticks who was wearing the wrong clothes and was ugly to boot.

But Edith never gave up. She was relentlessly cheerful. Her blue eyes, startling against her pale skin and dark hair, would sparkle and snap as she talked and talked about college, where she came from, people she met, teachers, and what they wanted, until finally Connie started to respond.

Later, Connie realized that Edith had been telling her what she needed to know to succeed. Doing it as if she was a chatterbox, but really she was a teacher. After Connie started talking and sharing, Edith stopped the constant chatter and became a listener instead. It was mostly because of Edith that Connie didn't give up, or go crazy, but instead started to feel at home.

So when Edith asked her to come home for Thanksgiving with her, Connie, having nowhere else to go, said yes with only the briefest moment of hesitation.

And in that way, she met the family that would not replace the women of King's Row but would become her new home. Until she ruined it.

But then, that day, sitting around the table with Edith, her parents, Ralph and Lorraine, and Edith's brother, Bill, she felt as if the world had finally opened its heart to her, and she was ready to say yes to living life with the same light heart as her friend Edith.

FIVE

After meeting Edith's family for the first time, Connie's desire to be someone important kicked into high gear. That drive to achieve was what had kept her sane growing up. It had stopped her from falling into the trap of her father's life.

Now that she had found her footing, she felt ready to conquer the world. And the place to start was where she was, in college.

She decided that every class she took was equally essential. Because each one would take her one step further away from the poverty she had known growing up. It didn't matter what the subject of the class was. She tackled it as if her life depended on it, which, to Connie, it did.

She had no time for a social life. She had never been a fan of what seemed to her to be silly games or talking about things that didn't matter. Now she had even less time for what she saw as wasting time. Her life revolved around work, going to classes, studying, and eating when she remembered to or when Edith brought her food.

One exception was the late-night talks she had with Edith about what they wanted to achieve in life. Alone in their dorm room, their hair in curlers, sitting cross-legged on their beds, walls covered with posters, clutter everywhere, and wearing college t-shirts that hung to their knees, they talked about what they would do after graduation.

They often disagreed. For Connie, going to college was the stepping-off point to doing anything she wanted to do, and although she hadn't decided exactly what that would be yet, she knew she would be the best at it.

Connie couldn't understand why Edith wanted so little and would ask her why she was at college, anyway. Edith would laugh and say it was fun and gay, and something to remember when she got married and had kids.

"Oh my God," Connie would scream at her, "That's all you want? What about being somebody? Making money?"

"No," Edith would answer, shaking her head so hard that her shiny dark hair would swing side to side, "That's not what is important to me."

Connie would huff, roll her eyes, and flop back on her bed in exasperation. She had not yet realized that she was the one out of step with the times. Edith was following the rules and social norms expected of them. Connie was not.

But she was too busy making her way through school to notice. Even if she had, she wouldn't have cared. She had bigger plans than marriage and children.

In fact, she had no plans for them at all. She had seen what marriage and children did to the women of the trailer park. It was not what they wanted for her, and it was not what she wanted for herself.

But it was their differences that made life better for both of them. Edith's ability to meet people and her cheerfulness kept Connie from falling into pits of depression over not being the best in the class, or by the mind-numbness of work.

In return, Connie helped Edith study for tests and raise her grades enough that her parents had stopped worrying that their daughter would never make it through school. Edith was grateful.

She could stay in college and get what she wanted. She had her eye on some of the boys in her class.

Edith was determined to marry someone like her father. Someone who would be an excellent family provider, and adore his wife, the same way her father adored her mother.

Edith never told Connie all of that, though. She knew that Connie would think that was stupid and rant and rail at her to change her mind. Instead, Edith thanked Connie in every way she could think of for helping her through school.

She was grateful that although Connie was her friend, she wasn't like her, because Connie's intense need to be someone and be the best was sometimes exhausting to be around.

Besides, she knew that none of the boys she had her eye on would like a woman like Connie. They were looking for women just like her. Ready and willing to be wives and mothers.

On the weekends, Edith could sometimes get Connie to take a walk through town with her. They would stroll in and out of the stores that lined the downtown streets. Many of the stores catered primarily to the college students and anyone who wanted to get gear that said "Penn State."

It was where they had picked up their man-sized Penn State t-shirts for nightwear, and when there were clearance sales, they added sweatshirts and t-shirts to wear during the day. Connie almost always said no to buying things. She had to save her money. But one time got a baseball cap with a lion on the front and she wore it all the time to remind herself that she was a lion at heart.

Edith would often treat Connie as a thank you for her tutoring. So after window shopping, they would head to Murphy's Five and Dime and have ice cream sundaes at the lunch counter. It was one of the few times that Connie would allow herself to laugh and giggle in public.

Edith told Connie that she was the sister she always wanted, and Connie told her the same was true for her.

Connie was making that up. She had never actually wanted a sister or a sibling of any kind. She thought it was lucky that her parents hadn't gotten around to having more children since they weren't fit to raise a child. A drunk, abusive father and a missing mother did not speak highly of their parenting abilities.

But she didn't want to hurt Edith's feelings. Technically, it was true because if she had known what it was like to have a best friend and a sister, she would have wanted one growing up.

During their first year of school, Connie went home with Edith over Christmas and spring break, and when Edith invited her to come home and spend the summer with her, Connie jumped at the chance, but with the caveat that she needed to work to earn money. Edith promised her there would be plenty of jobs.

It was during that summer that two things happened that moved Connie's life onto a path that would force her to make a decision that now, in death sitting alone in her empty house, she wondered if it had been the right one.

SIX

The house was so quiet. Connie thought she would go out of her mind. What had she been thinking when she was alive, staying in the house, not being part of life for so many years? Now, not being able to talk to anyone made her crazier than she had ever felt in life.

A few prospects had come through the house in the past few days to see if they wanted to buy it. Thankfully, it was the realtor who brought them through and not her daughter.

Connie didn't think she could handle hearing Karla describe the rooms as if nothing of any importance had ever happened in the house. Which wasn't true at all, she was sure. But then, for the life of her—*what a funny term,* she thought to herself—she couldn't remember what they might have been.

The house was familiar, but her life wasn't. It was slipping out of her grasp. Which was terrifying, but she had no idea what to do to stop it. What would she become when she didn't remember anything? What was she now?

The last time the realtor brought a young couple to the house, she had described it as a lovely starter home. When the couple asked what had happened to the woman who owned the house, she heard the realtor say that she had died, but the rest of her words had faded out, and Connie hadn't heard how she had died. In her sleep? Was that it?

That was what she thought had happened. Hadn't she gone to bed and then woke up like this? Dead?

Questions with no answers bounced around in Connie's head like ping pong balls. *If someone bought the house, would she stay? Why? Would she be stuck here forever?*

At the moment, Connie couldn't think of where else to go. If she had thought death would bring her a measure of peace, she had been wrong. She had none.

She was tired and couldn't sleep. Hungry and couldn't eat. She could pretend to lie down on the bed or sit on the swing on the porch, but nothing in her life was touchable. She hovered over everything. She was not gone and not present. The irony of it didn't escape her.

As she asked herself those questions, standing at the kitchen window looking out at the backyard and garden, Connie saw something that made her think that not only was she dead, but probably she had gone crazy too.

A boy was standing in the yard, staring at the house. Something about him seemed familiar, but she couldn't place it. She had never allowed children in her yard. Why was he there? Could she scare him away? She was a ghost, after all. Maybe she could be a scary ghost and get rid of him.

Habit, she told herself.

She had developed a habit of hiding in life, and now that she was dead, she was tired of it. She was dead tired of it—no more hiding. The boy was staring at the kitchen window, which meant that possibly he could see her. She raised her hand and waved with the tips of her fingers.

The boy didn't move. Had he seen her or not? A second later, he was gone.

"Come back," she said to no one because even when she was speaking out loud, she didn't think her voice sounded in the world. Having no one to test it on, she wasn't sure. And since the boy had vanished, she couldn't test it out on him.

The possibility that he hadn't been there passed through her mind, but she was unwilling to accept it. She wasn't that crazy. She wasn't making up things just to see them, and for sure, she wouldn't make up a boy in the yard.

Still not being used to being able to walk through the walls, she went around the kitchen cabinets and walked through the door instead. She couldn't touch it to open it, but it felt better to walk through a door. Made her feel more human, or real, even though she knew she wasn't anymore.

Looking around the yard, she could see no sign of the boy but noted that the garden seriously needed weeding, and the bird feeders were empty. Two things she had enjoyed doing in life, she realized. Had she noticed that she liked them when she was alive, or did she think of them as only chores to do during the day?

Thinking of gardening took her back to the summer with Edith at her family home, where she had first been introduced to gardens and birds by Edith's mother, Lorraine.

What a glorious summer it had been. Because Edith knew that Connie needed to work to earn money for school, Edith had talked her father into hiring Connie as a part-time assistant.

Edith thought it would be the perfect opportunity for Connie because she knew that Connie wanted to learn all about business, and her father was an accountant for almost everyone in town.

It hadn't taken much to convince Edith's father, Ralph. He liked Connie, and although he had wanted to work with Edith, she had refused. To Edith, what her dad did was boring. Instead, she took a part-time job as a lifeguard at the town's outdoor pool.

Edith's father told her to call him Ralph and even gave her a desk of her own at his office.

Connie couldn't believe how interesting the job was for her. Not the numbers or the filling out of spreadsheets and doing budgets, but learning how businesses worked.

Ralph was the accountant for many of the small companies in town, and when he found out how much Connie loved to hear about how those businesses operated, he let her sit in on many of the conversations.

It was her job to take notes, get coffee, put the papers in order, and retrieve files. None of what she did was important, but the words and what they talked about lit up Connie's life, and for the first time that she could remember, she was entirely happy.

Because both of their jobs were part-time, she and Edith had plenty of time to hang out by the pool, or ride bikes, or lie in the hammock in the backyard reading books. Edith's calm and happy family life provided Connie with a new understanding of why Edith might want to choose that kind of life.

But it didn't change her mind about what she wanted. She wanted to be like Edith's father. Not the family side of him. The business side.

She wanted to run her own business, be her own boss, make her own way in life, have people talk about her because she had achieved something on her own. There would be no family life for her. She would borrow Edith's, but not create her own.

SEVEN

The next day the boy appeared again. This time he was sitting in the grass looking at the oak tree in the backyard. At one point, when Karla was little, it had a swing attached to it. But Connie had taken it down long ago.

Even if Karla had children of her own, she wouldn't have brought them to her mother's house to play. That was something that Connie knew for sure, and until now, had told herself that she didn't care.

Now, seeing the boy outside staring at the tree, Connie had a momentary sense of panic. Was all of this some kind of test?

As far as she could tell, she had been dead for two weeks now, and still, there had been no contact from anyone, other than this boy, who hadn't actually contacted her. He just appeared out of nowhere.

Was she supposed to do something with him so she could leave this in-between place? She was dead, and she wasn't. She was thinking, feeling, and seeing things. That was life, wasn't it?

Connie decided that it had to be a test. Because if that was what was happening, all she had to do was pass it. Then maybe she could move on to somewhere else.

She didn't know where that somewhere was, but it had to be better than the waiting and not knowing.

I used to be good at tests, Connie thought. Even though she had no idea if she was right or not, or what the outcome would be if she passed it, Connie decided to throw herself into it.

She would assume that the little boy was a crucial part of her test. It was time to stop moping around. She had spent too much of her life doing that. Perhaps it was time to be like she used to be—brave, confident, and sure of herself.

Back in the trailer park, she had pretended to be those things. It had gotten her out of that life. If she did it again, perhaps it would bring her out of this in-between state.

Taking a deep breath—out of habit because no air passed through her body—Connie moved through the kitchen door and onto the lawn. The boy stood, turned, and looked at her, nodded his head, and disappeared. Again.

This time Connie knew that he had seen her, and a flare of hope rose in her heart. Someone had seen her. It didn't matter that it was only a boy, and it almost didn't matter that he kept disappearing. She had been seen. It was a beginning.

There was nothing that she could do to bring him back. Her only choice was to wait for him to return, which meant she had to stay at the house because she had no idea if the boy was attached to the home or not.

The house was probably part of the test too. Because just as she had never dreamed of starting a family or owning a house, she had done both.

Yes, it was time to revisit her life. Perhaps that would give her a clue an idea of what test she was in, and how to pass it. No, that is not the right attitude, she told herself. She would ace it. She would be like she was before, not like what she had become.

• • • ● ● • ● • ● • • •

That first summer opened up a whole new world for Connie, and as a result, she decided that she would study every aspect of Edith's life. Everything about the way they lived was entirely different from what she had known.

The most obvious was that they had a house, not a trailer. The trailer she grew up in would have fit into their living room. Actually, Edith's bedroom was larger than their trailer.

Instead of a shelf to sleep on, it had twin beds and was entirely pink. When Edith first showed her the room, Connie started laughing, partly because it was delightful in a weird way, but also to disguise the rush of envy that she felt. How many shades of pink could there be? And two beds? Why two beds?

Edith had said that the other bed was for sleepovers. Connie had sat on one bed and wondered how life could be so different for some people. What she thought of as sleepovers were the men who fell asleep drunk on the floor of their trailer, so she had to step over them to get out, being careful not to be caught or tripped on purpose by one of them.

To Edith, it was girls eating snacks, laughing, talking about boys, curlers in the hair, and playing Roy Orbison on the record player over and over again. It was being told by her parents to keep it down, but not really meaning it, and her brother Bill banging on the walls to be quiet but secretly enjoying that the house was filled with his sister's beautiful friends.

Every day that first summer was a revelation about life in a middle-class family. Connie ate food she had never heard of before, sang songs around the piano in the living room, and went to drive-in movies with Edith and Bill.

But it was the time at Ralph's office that showed her what she could do with her life. She learned to appreciate that knowing how businesses operated, and where their money went, gave Ralph power. Knowledge of what went on behind the scenes was essential. Ralph knew more about some people's businesses than they knew about it themselves.

When one of the car dealers came to Ralph, Ralph—as he insisted Connie call him—decided it would be a perfect test case for Connie to learn about how his business worked. At first, she hated it.

The dealer's company was a mess. He had receipts and bills in cardboard boxes. He didn't understand where the money came from or where it went. He hadn't filed taxes for years.

Later, Connie realized that Ralph wanted her to see the worst of it, and had chosen that business because it made her learn by starting at the beginning. She came to love it. She only had to see what Ralph was teaching her once, and she understood. By the time the summer was over, Connie felt as if she could have run the car dealer's business.

Ralph had told his entire family—actually anyone that would listen—that Connie was a natural. He would bet on her being a success at anything she did. And he told her that if all else failed, which he doubted would happen, she always had a job with him. If she wanted it, after she graduated, he would make her his partner. She was that good.

To Edith's credit, she didn't resent her father's decision or feel jealous. Instead, Edith, like the rest of her family, rejoiced that Connie had found a place in their family.

To Edith, that meant they would stay best friends forever, and that was important to her. Important enough to do what Connie asked her to do, even when she didn't want to.

Now, Connie, hovering in her garden, unable to do anything at all, wondered if this test was about what had happened to Edith.

And that it had been her fault.

She knew it then and had told herself that she didn't care. But perhaps she had cared after all. That thought was almost more terrifying than the knowledge that she was dead.

EIGHT

"Always running," that should have been my motto in life, Connie thought. *At first, running toward what she wanted, and then later running away from what she had done.*

"How did that go for you?" a voice asked from behind her.

Connie grabbed her chest, thinking if she wasn't already dead, the shock might have killed her. She whirled around to see the boy from the yard.

"Well, not all that well, if you must know," Connie answered with a snap of anger.

The two of them stared at each other, sizing each other up. Once again, Connie had the feeling that she might have met the boy before. He looked vaguely familiar.

She guessed that the boy was about ten, although she wasn't good at figuring how old adults were, let alone children. Now that he was standing close to her, she could see he had dark blue eyes and shiny black hair. He had on jeans, sneakers, and a t-shirt that looked too big for him. She waited for him to say something. He stared back at her. Finally, giving up on the boy saying something else, she asked, "Are you dead, too?"

The boy tilted his head to the side before replying, "Are you?"

Despite finally having someone to talk to, Connie felt like walking away. Just what she needed, a smart-ass little boy in her life. Connie hadn't wanted to be around kids before, and now the only person who saw her was this little monster.

But then she reminded herself that this was probably a test, and that meant she had to do something different. Feel something different.

The boy waited while she asked herself how she felt, and Connie realized that she felt angry. Very angry. But at who, and why, she wasn't sure. But this boy couldn't be the focus of her anger, could he?

So stop acting so self-righteous, she told herself.

While all that thinking was going on, the boy stood watching her. When she cleared her throat to speak, he smiled, which disabled her good intentions, and instead, she snapped, "What are you smiling about? Do you like dead old women?"

"Not really. And you died long before you stopped breathing."

Connie didn't have a snappy answer to that one. Instead, she turned away and stared at the oak tree the way the boy had before.

In her mind's eye, Connie saw her daughter, Karla, sitting on the swing that hung from one of the tree's branches and calling out to her to push her. She hadn't.

Instead, she had pretended not to hear her and kept her attention on pruning the rosebush that had started climbing up one of the screens in the back of the house.

"Mom, mom," Karla had called and then stopped.

Looking back, Connie knew that Karla had decided that day to stop asking her mother for help.

At the time, Connie had thought Karla was growing up and didn't need her as much, but now she saw what had really happened. Karla had decided to find somewhere else to get the attention she needed and stop begging for it from the mother who wouldn't give it to her.

Turning back to the boy who had stood waiting for her, Connie asked the question she was afraid to get the answer to, "Are you here to help me?"

"If you want it," the boy answered.

This time Connie didn't turn away. "I want it."

"No matter what it takes or how hard it will be?"

Connie hesitated. Could things be worse than they were? What if she failed? Would she go to some kind of hell worse than this?

"Can you guarantee that I won't fail at whatever this is we are doing?"

"Can you guarantee that you will keep trying no matter what happens?"

"Trying what?" Connie snapped back.

The boy disappeared.

Two days later, he came back—actually forty-nine hours and thirty-one minutes later, to be precise. Connie knew. She had stared at the kitchen clock, counting the hours, wondering if he would ever return.

During that time, the realtor had returned with the couple looking for their starter home. After touring the house again, they made an offer. Connie knew what that meant. Her time was running out in the home.

There was no way she would stay around and watch people take over the house. Even though she didn't like it—never had liked it—it had been their home for many years.

The only thing she had liked about it was the garden and the birds.

"Please," she asked whoever was listening, "If there is someone out there, bring the boy back. And let the people who buy this house like gardens and birds."

Connie's hopes were raised when the woman had noticed the butterfly bush blooming in the yard. She had told her husband about it as they walked to their car. She knew plants. It might be okay for the garden.

Connie knew it was a silly thing to care about. She should be more worried about her future. But what could she do about it without help? So she checked the kitchen clock every thirty minutes.

Did people pay attention to the time when they were dead? They must. She was dead, and yet she still watched the time and counted the days.

Did the little boy do the same thing? Did he watch the sunrise and sunsets to notice the passing of days the same way that she was doing?

Why she bothered, she didn't know. Nothing changed in this new way of being. She was nowhere in space and nowhere in time, and she had chased away the one and only person who could see her and who claimed he could help.

What difference was it that he was just a kid? Finally, when she couldn't take it any longer, she stood in the empty kitchen and yelled. "I'll do it. Whatever it takes."

She could barely hear her voice as she yelled. Was it like the tree in the forest—unless someone is there to listen to it when it falls, is it soundless? If no one could hear her, was she voiceless?

Nothing happened the first ten times she yelled it. On the eleventh try, the boy appeared, holding his hands over his ears.

"Stop it!" He yelled back. "I heard you the first time, but you aren't the only thing I have going on."

Connie just stared at him, unsure what to say or think, afraid she might offend him. Carefully she asked, "What do you mean by that? What else do you have going on?"

The boy let out a sigh that held no breath and said, "I mean, you are not the only dead person who needs help."

"So you are confirming that I am dead. And that I need help," Connie asked, smiling at him.

She wondered if that was the first time she had smiled since she died. And then she wondered when was the last time she had smiled, dead or alive.

NINE

She had smiled a lot in the summer of 1965. Even now, the memory of it made her smile. That summer had been magical. There were days when she had felt as if she would split apart with happiness. While living in the trailer park, she could never have imagined feeling as happy as she had that summer.

Each member of the family played a part in making each day perfect. Connie's hours at Ralph's office filled her head with thoughts about making money and becoming someone. She knew now that she would like to run her own business. Ralph encouraged that idea but suggested that she explore all her options before deciding.

"That's what college is for," he told her. "It's where you can learn how to think and discover yourself."

Connie didn't want to tell him that it was not what Edith wanted from college. She thought Ralph probably already knew, and she didn't want to probe what might be a sore spot. Besides, she was delighted that both Bill and Edith had no desire to learn what Ralph had to teach. They were happy to have Connie take their spot.

Edith was in her element and delighted in sharing it with

Connie. Edith dragged Connie to the pool whenever she could and taught her how to swim. Connie knew how to swim, but it looked like what Edith called dog paddling.

Pools were entirely new to Connie. There had been a lake near her, but she had no way to get to it. Besides, the women told her to stay out of it. "It's dirty," was the only thing they had said.

The pool, on the other hand, smelled like chlorine, so she felt it was clean. Forever after that, the smell of chlorine would take her back to that time. If she allowed herself, she would pretend that she was still there, living in Edith's world.

Her time at the pool gave her a tan and blond streaks in her hair. She liked the look. She learned to love real swimming. She enjoyed the feeling of slicing through the water. Being the person she was, she soon became addicted to swimming laps. Doing more each day was another way to achieve something.

Edith chose a different thing to do at the pool. On her off hours, she would sit on their towel and hold court over the boys who would try to win her attention and favors.

Connie would look over at Edith, surrounded by boys, and laugh, and Edith would wink back. What those boys didn't know was that none of them would win Edith's heart. They were practice sessions for Edith. She was learning more skills to win over the boys she had her sights set on, the ones back in college.

Connie had no desire to join in that kind of game. Even if she was interested, she had many mothers back at King's Row who would be disappointed in her.

Because Connie was not only achieving for herself. She was doing it for them. She swore that someday she would repay them for giving her a chance at a better life. In the meantime, she had things to do. Besides, she had yet to meet any boy who wanted things more out of life than she did.

Except maybe Bill. As the older brother, Bill was happy that Connie was Edith's friend. Some days they would sit on the porch swing together and talk about what they wanted in life.

Bill was as handsome as Edith was beautiful, and for a brief moment, Connie had considered that Bill might make a good first boyfriend.

But that moment had passed. Instead, they became good friends, which Connie soon realized was far more valuable. Bill had one more year of college as an architecture major and was actively looking for a job in the city.

"What city?" Connie had asked. And he answered, "Any city."

Bill wanted to get away from the small-town life as much as Connie wanted to be somebody. But Connie didn't think it was because he wanted to be someone like she did. It felt more like he had a secret, and a city was where he could hide it.

Towards the end of the summer, Connie thought she had figured out his secret and wanted to ask him, but was afraid asking him would ruin their friendship.

She also thought Bill's mother, Lorraine, knew what it was, but she was afraid to talk about it for the same reason. Or maybe she thought it would make it real if she said it out loud.

Lorraine taught Connie about gardens and birds. When Lorraine wasn't in the kitchen making their meals, Connie would often find her outside on her hands and knees weeding or planting.

Lorraine belonged to the local garden club, and their house was on the list of gardens to visit that year. When Connie found out why she was working so hard in the garden, she volunteered to help.

The moment Loraine handed her a pair of gloves and a trowel, Connie was hooked.

It was an odd thing to like, Connie realized. She planned to take over some part of the world. Why waste time working in the garden and feeding birds when that was not on a career pathway? Gardening and birds would not help her achieve her goals in life.

But later, Connie was happy that she had found them because

her love for them had helped her survive more than one trauma. Even when she had moved to the city to build her career, she always had pots of plants and bird feeders.

Yes, that summer had provided her with more happiness in a few short months than all the years of her life until then. She carried that summer around with her as a jewel that sparkled with perfect memories.

Every member of that family had given her something that changed her in ways so profound that it took her years to acknowledge it.

It was what she had done that changed their lives that made her a terrible person.

At that moment, Connie knew who the boy reminded her of, and once again, she felt as if she would die of a heart attack.

Except she was already dead. And so was Edith's little boy, Eddie.

TEN

Connie's knees buckled, and she fell to the ground. And even though she was not actually on the ground, she bent over and buried her face in the grass, hoping she could smell it and make this horrible dream go away. She couldn't. And it didn't.

Eddie laughed. "Caught you by surprise, didn't I?"

Connie sat back and looked at him. Sitting on top of the grass, she was about the same height as him, and his dark blue eyes twinkled as he laughed at her.

"I don't think it's funny or something to laugh about. What's wrong with you, anyway? You're dead. What's there to laugh about?"

"Now, that's where you are wrong, Miss Connie," Eddie said, twirling in a circle, arms in the air as if he were a leaf spinning in the wind.

"Where am I wrong?" Connie demanded, trying and mostly failing to get herself under control.

"Well, I could say you've been wrong about everything for years, but I don't need to tell you that. You have had time to think about what you did with your life.

"I mean that you might be wrong about there not being

something to laugh about and that I am dead."

Connie stood up and looked down at the boy.

"You are dead. I heard about it."

"And you didn't come to the funeral, did you?"

"I never go to funerals," Connie shot back.

Both of them stopped and didn't speak. Eddie waited so that Connie could hear what she had just said.

When she turned and walked back towards the house, he followed.

"Go away," Connie said.

"Even though I am the only one you can talk to? Are you sure you want to tell me to go away? What if I never come back and you are stuck here forever? Because you will be.

"And the other thing that you are wrong about is thinking I am dead—because I am not. At least not in the same way that you are dead."

"What makes you different?"

Connie faced Eddy, hands on her hips, trying to take control of the situation, and then, realizing that she would never have control of this situation, started to cry.

Eddy didn't wait for her to stop crying before replying, "It's pretty obvious. I can come and go."

With those words, Eddy vanished, leaving Connie feeling as if her insides had been ripped out and put on display.

She thought things were bad before, but they had just gotten worse.

• • • ● ● • ● • ● • •

Eddie came back a few hours later. Connie hadn't moved. She

had stood in front of the clock and watched the minutes tick by, wondering why the world kept going the same way as before, even if she wasn't part of it.

And she let the tears roll down her face because it was true; she hadn't been part of the world long before she died.

While she watched the clock tick, she let herself return to when she had been alive, really alive, that summer with Edith and her family, and what they had done for her.

All summer, she had been worried whether she would have enough money to finish school. But then Edith's family had changed everything.

One morning Ralph and Lorraine had sat Connie down at the kitchen table and told her they had to talk to her about something. She was terrified that she had done something wrong, and would have to leave.

Instead, Ralph said that they had paid her next year's tuition and room and board. And they said that they would help her apply for scholarships and loans, and with the promise that if she kept on working both at school and her jobs, they would make sure she always had enough.

When she tried to refuse, they wouldn't let her. Instead, Ralph and Lorraine told her she was like a daughter to them. Both Edith and Bill were happier because Connie was in their life, and Ralph said his business had never been more organized.

"Besides," Ralph had said, "Paying for your next year of school is an investment for us. All we want in return is for you to be part of our family."

For Connie, it was as if heaven had opened its doors. Not only did she have the women of the trailer park believing in her, but an entire family.

It didn't matter that this family wasn't related to her; they had accepted her as if they were—not like the mother she never knew, and the father she never wanted to see again.

"You told her?" Edith had said, bouncing into the kitchen as the three of them sat at the table, holding hands with overflowing eyes.

Right behind Edith was Bill, who said, "Oh, good. You said yes, didn't you?"

Connie could only nod. She stood and hugged Edith and Bill. She had a brother and a sister—something she had never thought she would want or have.

"Let's celebrate," Ralph had shouted.

"Pancakes!" Edith had responded.

After that, anytime Edith and Connie wanted to celebrate something, they always went for pancakes.

Back in her kitchen watching the clock, Connie smiled at the memory and then shivered. She hadn't touched pancakes for years. She never made them. Never went to eat them, even when Karla had begged for them.

No matter how hard she had tried, she could never erase the memory of the Matthews family as they celebrated that day that she became a daughter in their family.

Hours later, when Eddie returned, as she knew he would, Connie turned to him and said, "I'm ready. I will do whatever I need to do."

Eddie cocked his head to the side, studying her. Finally, he answered. "Okay. Then it's time for you to meet someone."

A second later, Connie was no longer in her kitchen, and she and Eddie were no longer alone.

ELEVEN

Bryan Anderson loved walking in the woods. It didn't matter the season. To him, it was always beautiful. Even in the winter, he loved it. The naked tree branches against the sky were so beautiful he could, and did, spend hours studying their design. And it was people-quiet in the winter. He rarely encountered anyone on the trails with their noisy walking and chattering.

Instead, his companions were animals and birds. Deer and rabbits would often find him during his walks. The deer would stand in the undergrowth by the trail and watch him walk by, barely moving. Only a flick of their ears would give them away.

Bryan would say hello and stand as still as they did. They would stare at each other, and Bryan would imagine that the deer was talking to him. When the deer stomped his feet, Bryan thought it meant the deer was ready to leave, so Bryan would clasp his hands together at his heart and bow to the deer. He believed that the deer would tip his head in return.

Today Bryan was so lost in thought he barely noticed the changes that were occurring all around him. Winter had given way to spring a few weeks earlier, and now the little buds on all the tree branches were silhouetted against the sky. Spring wildflowers had begun to bloom, and the willow's green leaves had already appeared. Bryan barely noticed. He was preoccupied with what was happening with him. What he called "the problem" was getting worse. Or better, he thought to himself, depending on his point of view.

And that was another problem. Bryan didn't know if he liked or hated what was happening.

There was a rustle in the bushes beside the path, and a rabbit hopped out in front of him. Bryan laughed. He knew this rabbit. They were walking friends and had been for many years, ever since Brian was a boy who escaped to the woods.

They had walked together for so many years that Bryan knew that it couldn't be the same rabbit. But he figured that somehow they had passed the job down from rabbit to rabbit, so he thought of them as the same one.

Today the rabbit did what it always did. Stared at him. And when Bryan took a step forward, the rabbit began hopping down the trail, leading the way. The rabbit would slow down or speed up or even wait, depending on what Bryan would do.

Sometimes they would walk that way for hours. When Bryan turned around to head home, the rabbit would dart in front of him and walk, or in his case, hop back until they reached what Bryan assumed was the rabbit's home, because it would scuttle into the bush, turn, give Bryan one last look, and then disappear into the underbrush.

Today, Bryan didn't have time to walk too far. He was meeting a friend for lunch at the Diner. He was debating whether he would tell her about what had been happening to him. Would telling her help or make it worse? Either way, telling her meant he had to admit that it was real.

The problem had started when he moved back home to the small house on the outskirts of Doveland to take care of his mother. She had asked him to, and he had said yes. How could he not? There was no one else to do it. Besides, he had nothing keeping him in the city. No proper job, no family.

He could blame the fact that nothing ever went right for him or his parents, but he knew it wasn't their fault. They had both done their best with a boy who couldn't focus. As long as he could remember, he only wanted to walk in the woods. These woods. They had been his secret home away from home. But the woods hadn't helped him get through school. Not that he wanted to fail at school. He simply couldn't get himself to care enough about it to do well.

So he had squeaked through high school, kissed his parents goodbye, and moved to the city hoping that would cure him of his daydreaming. He got a job. First, as a dishwasher in a restaurant and eventually making his way up to being a waiter at a restaurant that did well enough that he could pay his rent for a room in an apartment owned by one of the cooks. He ate well. That's the best he could say about his life.

The few times he visited his parents, he did his best not to let the woods draw him back in. His parents thought he was distancing himself from them when he would leave days earlier than he promised, but what he was doing was running from the call of the forest path. When his father passed away from a heart attack five years ago, he came home for the funeral, stayed a few days, and left again before his mother discovered what a failure he had become.

He always lied to them about his work. He borrowed pieces of conversations he heard when waiting on tables and used that information to convince his parents he was successful at all the vague jobs he would mention. They would smile and nod and tell him they loved him. Maybe he would like to come back to Doveland?

"No," he'd say, "They need me at work."

His mother would bite her lip, and he knew she was trying not to cry, trying to keep herself from begging him to come home.

A few weeks after his father died, he received a check in the mail. His father had left him some money. In the envelope was a note his father had written to him and left with the lawyer. It invited him to go home and walk in the woods.

Bryan broke down. He had never fooled his father, and of course, that meant his mother had always known, too. And now she had died, too, and he had no one.

As Bryan walked, he scuffed his feet, leaving a trail in the dust. Turning around, Brian looked back at it and thought about how the life you lived followed you just like the scrapes in the dirt. For him, there were no clear footprints, no direction, just feet dragging through everything.

His mother had left him three gifts. She had left him the house, and she left him the rest of their savings account. In it was enough so he could live comfortably if he stayed in the house. He could walk in the woods for the rest of his life.

But she left him one more thing. And that was the thing he called the problem.

What was hard for him to admit was perhaps, if he wasn't crazy, the gift his mother had left him gave his life a purpose. God only knew how much he needed a purpose in life.

Yes, he would tell Rachel about the problem, and if she believed him, that would mean he wasn't crazy.

He had gone to school with Rachel. Sometimes they had walked in the woods together. She had never laughed at him, even when her friends teased her for befriending such a loser.

She had come to both his father and his mother's funeral. A few weeks after his mother's funeral, she started calling him, inviting him to breakfast.

He always turned her down. Until yesterday, when he had said yes.

Following his scuff marks back down the trail, rabbit leading the way, Bryan thought, *yes, perhaps it is time to start living.*

The irony of it was that if he wasn't crazy, he would begin to live by helping the dead.

TWELVE

"Where are we?" Connie asked, grabbing Eddie's arm in fear.

"You've been here," Eddie replied. "You know where you are."

"No!" Connie shouted. "I don't want to be here. Take me home."

"No, I won't. You ran from this your entire life, and now you are still trying to run even though you are dead. You agreed. Now you are here. I could leave you here to deal with it on your own, or I can help. Those are your only choices."

Connie looked around where Eddie had brought her and remembered how beautiful it had been to her the summers she had lived with Edith's family. Until she left them and broke everyone's heart. Including her own.

When Connie turned and walked away, Eddie walked away too. He had someone to see first anyway, and it would give Connie the chance to think about her life, which is what Connie had decided to do.

Eddie's threat that he would leave her there didn't worry Connie. She knew he wouldn't, just as she knew he was right. She had to stay and deal with what she had done.

She and Edith had returned to college after that wonderful first summer. Ralph and Lorraine had paid her tuition and dorm fees, as they had promised. She sent a thank-you card to them and a letter to her trailer park women telling them that all was well. She told them she was still in school and was very happy.

In her mind's eye, she could see the women gathering in one of the tiny trailers reading her letter while the kids ran around outside, and their husbands and boyfriends worked or drank what they earned.

Connie had yearned to do something for them, and that desire drove her to get even better grades. She had changed her major to business. Not for Ralph, but because of him.

The next few years flew by. Every holiday Connie went home with Edith and strengthened her friendship with Bill. He had moved to Pittsburgh but always returned for the holidays and a few weeks every summer. At school, Edith got passing grades and collected men while Connie got A's and collected information.

At the beginning of their third year of college, Connie had moved into an apartment with Edith. Located over one of the stores downtown, it was small, but cozy and ideally located for each of them—for different reasons.

Edith loved the separate bedrooms. She made good use of hers while trying to decide which boy she was dating was the one. Connie loved watching the flow of students and townspeople as they shopped and strolled through the streets and up onto the campus.

It was the summer after they graduated that both Edith and Connie disappointed Ralph and Lorraine. But not in the same way. Edith had chosen a boy, and Connie had accepted a job.

The boy's name was Theodore Prince. Theo came from a family with money and had a built-in future that included a job at his families' business, which he was destined to run someday.

Connie understood why Edith had chosen him. Theo was

everything Edith had set out to get. He was handsome, in what Connie thought of as a stereotypical way, tall with dark hair that curled onto his collar. Connie thought the hairstyle was affected. It was a way to look rebellious and still be owned by tradition.

However, she agreed with Edith that Theo was charming. His dark brown eyes would warm slightly when he listened, and he always knew the right thing to say.

That quality irritated Connie the most. She figured that the only way he could be that charming all the time was that he worked at it. And that meant, to Connie, that he was faking it. Maybe it only covered a shallow interior which Connie rationalized that Edith wouldn't mind, as long as he provided her with what she wanted: home, family, and security.

But Connie worried that the charm hid more than that. She worried that Theodore Prince had gone searching for the perfect wife the same way Edith had searched for the perfect husband. She worried that Theo wanted a compliant woman who would keep his home and provide a family in exchange for what Connie saw as false security.

But Connie loved Edith, and Edith loved Theo, so she defended Edith's choice to Ralph and Lorraine. Ralph and Lorraine didn't want their daughter to move away, and that was their disappointment.

However, she didn't defend Edith's choice to Bill because Connie knew that Bill also worried about Theo and his motives. Still, she told Bill not to worry. She would continue to watch over Edith. At the time, they both thought that was possible.

Even though Connie and Edith were heading into two separate lives, Connie believed with all her heart that they would always be best friends and that their soul-sister status would never change.

Bill had shaken his head at Connie's optimism but said nothing. What could he say? That it was obvious what was coming? But not wanting to spoil his sister's happiness, he never let on how worried he was about her choice. Only much later did he share his feelings. But by then, it was too late.

They planned the wedding for the end of the summer of 1968 to accommodate Connie's plans to go to work at her new job in the fall. She was not working for Ralph. This was the way she had disappointed Ralph and Lorraine.

Connie had waited to tell Ralph and Lorraine one morning around the same kitchen table where they had first told her they would support her through school. Connie cried as she told them.

Lorraine had held her hand, and Ralph took a long moment before clearing his throat, and although his eyes filled with tears, he told her how proud he was of her. And his job offer was always open to her. But he understood that she wanted more than to be an accountant in a small town like Doveland.

When Edith and Bill came down to breakfast, only Bill knew that something had happened, but all three kept it to themselves. It was to be Edith's last summer at home, and they wanted it to be the best summer of her life.

Between planning for the picture-perfect wedding, and lengthy phone calls with Theo, Edith was never happier. Connie was happy too, but she knew that no matter what they said to each other about things not changing, there would never be another summer like this one again.

She was right. The trip she made back to Doveland after that summer never reached that level of joy. And then that terrible thing happened, and she never returned.

And now, here she was again. And once again, all she felt was sorrow and anger. But this time, Connie asked herself who was responsible for what had happened. She didn't like the answer, because all of it pointed back to her.

That was why Eddie had brought her back to Doveland. However, what she didn't understand was, now that she was dead, how could she do anything about it? Besides, that was in the past.

Nothing could change the past, could it?

THIRTEEN

The Diner hadn't changed much. Bryan knew that a husband and wife had bought the Diner a few years before and upgraded it, but they kept the general look of the Diner the same.

He found that reassuring. Because even though he had lost his parents, the town and the Diner still held their memories for him. He and his mom and dad had often had Sunday morning breakfasts at the Diner. His dad always made the same stupid joke. Sunday was a day for his wife to take a break from breakfast making. It wasn't amusing, but his mom would always laugh and squeeze his dad's hand.

At the time, their obvious love for each other made him uncomfortable. Now he envied them.

Rachel Windsor was waiting for him in the same booth they would meet in when they were kids. Like him, she had aged since their years in high school, but he thought she looked even more beautiful if that was even possible.

In his eyes, she had always been the most beautiful girl in school. That they were friends kept some taunting from the other boys at bay. If Rachel liked him, he couldn't be as big a wimp as he looked.

Maturity suited Rachel. On the other hand, he knew he hadn't aged well. Worry had put lines on Bryan's forehead, and dark circles around his eyes. Rachel's quickly disguised look of shock at seeing him told him it was probably worse than he thought.

After ordering, Rachel sipped at her drink and chatted about her garden and the town. He knew she was trying to lighten the mood, and when he barely answered her, she finally stopped, sat back against the seat of the booth, and asked him what was going on.

Taking a sip of water, Bryan gathered his courage and said, "It's mom."

Tipping her head to the side, Rachel looked over at her friend and asked, "Your mom? What about your mom?"

Seeing the compassion present in Rachel's blue eyes, he said, "I see her sometimes."

When Rachel didn't move but continued to listen, he added, "Not as much anymore. Mostly right after she died, she would come to tell me things.

"At first, I thought I was dreaming, but then it happened all the time. Sometimes she would appear out of nowhere and sit at the table, or out in the garden, and start talking.

"I know. It's crazy. And I probably would be okay with it if I just saw mom. I could figure that it's just my mind giving me memories of her because I miss her so much. And I was such a lousy son.

"She tells me all the time, just as she did when she was alive, that I'm not, or wasn't. Which is good. I am starting to believe that she and dad loved me anyway. So that's what I would think is happening, me trying to make sense of my life. Except…"

"Except what, Bryan," Rachel urged, reaching out and holding his hand on the table.

"Except now I see other people that are dead, too."

Many thoughts ran through Rachel's mind, wondering what words would be the right ones to say. Looking up, she saw Pete, the owner of the Diner, coming towards them with their food order, and she said, "Well, I am not surprised. After all, it's Doveland."

Releasing Bryan's hand, Rachel sat back so Pete could put the plate down. She smiled up at him, and then looked back to Bryan, who looked at her as if he had never seen her before.

"Come on," she said, gesturing at their food. "Eat up. It's delicious, and it looks as if you need to do some serious eating."

Rachel started up again on the chit chat while taking bites of food and smiling at Bryan, who, after realizing that was all she would say until they ate, had almost sucked up his food.

"I guess I was hungry," Bryan said, looking down at his empty plate.

Rachel licked the salt off her fingertips from the french fries and smiled. "Me, too. Now, do you want to tell me more, or was that it?"

"You mean it's not weird to you? And what do you mean, 'after all, it's Doveland?'"

"No, it's not weird to me. Actually, I'm a little jealous. I've always wanted to be able to see dead people, not scary ones, just people that I would like to have a conversation with.

"And as for Doveland. Well, since you left, people moved here that do some strange things. At least I've heard about them.

"You know I love listening in on conversations, and I overheard a few doozies that made me think some of our recent residents can do things the rest of us can't. So maybe they made room for this kind of thing to happen to you."

When Bryan said nothing, Rachel continued, "Did it start with your mom? Was she the first dead person you saw?"

Bryan nodded, "Yes. But then mom told me I could have done this all along if I hadn't been so afraid. So when she died, she opened the door for me because it worried her I would never get there on my own, beating myself up the way that I did. Or do."

Bryan paused, thinking about what he was saying. Rachel squeezed his hand and nodded at him to continue.

"Mom told me that there were people in what she called the in-between that could use my help."

"So, have you helped anyone yet?"

"Not really. I don't see that many, and most of them ignore me. But there is one boy that I've talked to, and he said he would bring me someone that needed my help.

"But, like I told mom, I don't understand how I'm supposed to help him. The boy said that he would show me. He would be my guide."

"What's the boy's name?"

"Eddie."

"Eddie? Eddie, who?"

"I don't know. I never asked his last name. But he looks like he is maybe ten years old."

"Well, find out his last name, then perhaps we can do some research about him, which might be helpful, especially if he lived here. Did he say who he was bringing and when?"

"No, he didn't," Bryan answered, as he glanced outside the window, and then added, "but it looks like it's a woman, and it might be now."

FOURTEEN

Rachel followed Bryan's gaze. He was looking across the street at the small park that sat in the center of the town. Spring had arrived, so a few people were sitting on the park benches, maybe waiting for someone to finish shopping, or just taking a moment to enjoy the fresh spring air.

None of them looked like a ghost to her. But then, she had no idea what a ghost looked like anyway. When the new people had come to town, rumors had spread that they could see people who had died, and they talked with people who visited from other dimensions.

Although Rachel believed that was possible, no amount of trying—which she did—produced anything other than drowsiness. She had given up trying, deciding that some people must have that talent, and others didn't. She obviously didn't.

But what she did have was a burning curiosity—about everything—which is why she listened in on conversations, read too many books for her own good, as her mother used to tell her, and researched the idea that some people could see people who had died. The word ghost was discouraged. She agreed. The word ghost made her think of Halloween and wearing white sheets with holes in them like they did when they were kids.

Either way, Rachel had decided neither to believe nor not believe. Instead, she would remain curious and open-minded. It seemed impossible to her that the universes could be only what they knew now.

I mean, after all, she would tell herself, *think of all the previously unknown things that science has discovered that were right in front of us all along. What else is there?*

Rachel could also not believe that she would one day vanish and never be seen again, just as she couldn't believe that all of creation popped into existence one day. No. She was curious, and she was logical. That version of creation made no sense. But what did? That's what interested her.

This was another reason she had always loved hanging out with Bryan. Sure, she dated lots of boys in high school. But Bryan was the one that stayed a constant. Probably because they hadn't dated. They were just friends.

He didn't chase after her and make her feel like some kind of prize to be acquired. Instead, he told her things. Why he loved the woods and the animals he knew. Like the rabbit. Rachel wondered if a rabbit still walked with him in the woods.

Bryan took her for many walks in the woods, showing her plants and trees, explaining what they were and how they lived, and how they collaborated. Rachel found it fascinating.

She found Bryan fascinating, too. In the woods, Bryan came alive. His blue eyes would flash, he'd run his hand through his sandy hair, little bits of twigs remaining in it, and she would think he was the most handsome boy she had ever seen.

But she was afraid to let him know how she felt. His friendship was too important to her. She was a person to him, not a body, not a conquest. She was the person he trusted. So she waited for him to make a move, hoping for something no matter how small, like holding her hand or a tiny kiss on the cheek.

Rachel dreamed about it and drew little stick figures of the two of them, hoping that maybe it would come true.

But it hadn't. Bryan had left the day after graduation, and even when he visited his parents, he never came to see her. So she gave up, married one of the boys who chased her, went to school part time and worked at a local real estate office. The marriage had lasted ten years—long enough for Rachel to know that she couldn't turn herself into what he wanted.

Instead, she wanted a career, and with the help of the people in the real estate office, eventually became a realtor on her own. Her husband hated that she was never home. And she hated to go home. Finally, they both knew they had probably never been a suitable match. He moved away, and for the past twelve years, she had remained happily single. She had thought of moving to a big city—more opportunity, make more money, meet more people.

She had even tried it for a few months. She had hated it—too much noise, too many cars, too many strangers. Besides, in the back of her head, she always thought that maybe, just maybe, someday Bryan would come home, and they would walk in the woods together again.

And now here he was. And her heart still beat a little faster when she looked at him. Despite the worry lines and the dark circles under his eyes, he was still beautiful to her. Rachel knew that men didn't want to be called beautiful, but it was what she saw in him. A beauty underneath all the worry that had always been there and still was.

Rachel knew that his parents had seen it too. But his parents didn't know how to help Bryan find his way in a world that rarely valued that kind of inner beauty and awareness. If Bryan didn't appreciate it in himself, how could he expect others to?

So, although Bryan hadn't yet invited her to walk in the woods, he had asked to see her. When he called, she had to work hard at not shouting "yes" at the invitation. Instead, she calmly said that she would love to.

She had expected little from the meeting. So the fact that he had shared his biggest secret and biggest fear with her made her happy, even though she could see the fear in him.

Rachel knew that he worried that perhaps he was crazy, and if so, what could he do about it. So she wanted to be able to look out the window and see what he saw. For him. For her.

But that wishing didn't make it happen. Instead, it was a typical view of the park. She saw people she knew, and none of them were dead. Although, she thought, perhaps she hadn't heard that they had died?

However, the woman who owned the coffeehouse across the street was handing out drinks to people on the bench, so they must be alive. Grace was like that, always reaching out. And Grace was most definitely alive, which meant so were the people on the benches, and the ones driving their cars around the park.

So she had to ask Bryan. "Who do you see?" and wait for his answer.

"Eddie and some woman. She doesn't appear thrilled with him, though."

"What happens now?" Rachel asked.

"Well, it appears that he wants me to come outside and talk with him. I know that you can't see him, but will you come with me?"

Bryan looked at Rachel and realized that she was already standing and had put money on the table. Her eyes were shining with delight.

"Come on. I can't wait to meet this Eddie. Even if I can't see him, you can tell me what he says."

Bryan felt as if a thousand-pound weight had been lifted off of his chest. Maybe it would be alright, after all.

What Bryan and Rachel didn't see as they left the Diner, was Pete watching them. He had heard what they said. It didn't surprise him, but at the next Monday night meeting, he would let them know. Just in case they could help.

FIFTEEN

Eddie saw Bryan heading his way along with a woman who was holding onto his arm as if she was stepping into something dangerous. Bryan was frowning, as always. Eddie knew that Bryan didn't like the unfamiliar world he had found himself in, especially his participation in it.

Bryan's mother, Jillyan, was the reason the door to the in-between had opened for him, and even though she had done Bryan a favor, he hadn't realized that yet.

Connie turned to look at the two people heading towards them and realized that the man was looking right at her. "That man sees me?" she whispered.

Eddie didn't answer Connie. It wasn't necessary, because Bryan had stopped in front of Eddie and asked, "Who is she?"

Before Eddie could answer, Bryan's friend had whispered something to him, and he looked at her as if she had lost her mind. But he did what she asked. Bryan turned to Eddie and said, "This is my friend Rachel Windsor, and Rachel, this is Eddie Prince and..?"

When Eddie said, "Connie Matthews," Bryan repeated her name to Rachel.

"Wait," Rachel said. "Eddie Prince? I know that name. Do I

know you from before?" Rachel asked, looking in the direction that she thought Eddie must be standing, but missing him by a few feet.

Eddie and Connie exchanged looks before Eddie answered. Since Rachel couldn't hear Eddie, Bryan relayed what he said.

"He said not to worry about that now."

Turning back to Eddie, Bryan asked, "Why are you here?"

"I brought you the first person you are going to help."

"Help? Help how?"

"This will take a little longer than we have standing here in the park while you look like a crazy person talking to the air.

"Grace over there is taking it in, and so is Pete. Go on home, and we'll meet you there later. I need to take Connie for a walk around the town before she settles into what she has to do.

"And as for your friend there, bring her along."

"But she can't see you, so how can she help?"

"She's going to help you, and you will need it."

Bryan looked back at the Diner, in time to see Pete walk away from the window and say something to a woman Eddie knew was Pete's wife, Barbara. Grace had her back to them, but Bryan knew that Eddie was right. Grace had heard him talking. Maybe she thought he was talking to Rachel, but he doubted it.

What kind of trouble was he in? Looking down at Rachel, Bryan knew that Eddie was right. He would need Rachel's help. Would she be willing to give it to him? After all, he had walked away from her before, pretending that he didn't need her. Maybe she wouldn't want to get involved with all this craziness.

But when she looked up at him, her green eyes curious and happy, and then smiled, he sighed. It was Rachel. She had always been there for him. Maybe it would be okay.

$$\bullet \ \bullet \ \bullet \ \bullet \ \bullet \ \bullet \ \bullet \ \bullet \ \bullet \ \bullet$$

Grace Strong watched Bryan and Rachel leave the park together. She knew about both of them. Not because she knew them, but because she had made it her business to know everyone in town. Grace loved that she was known as the town's busybody. As soon as she moved to Doveland a few years before, she had started into her favorite pastime, learning everything she could about everyone in town.

Setting up the town's favorite coffee shop, Your Second Home, gave her every opportunity to meet people. She wasn't a gossip. She was a listener. Her deep brown eyes never strayed as she listened.

Grace knew that she was not, and never had been, a beautiful woman, and now that she was older, her short and stocky frame fit everyone's version of a sweet old lady. But everyone who knew her understood that Grace was much more than she looked. They knew she was always aware, always paying attention to the world and people around her. It was inevitable that Grace would overhear Bryan's conversation with apparently no one.

She had smiled to herself, thinking that perhaps another interesting story was about to unfold in Doveland. As Grace headed back to her shop, she saw Pete standing in the Diner's window and waved to him. She knew that he had waited for her to see him. It meant that he had noticed something too about Bryan and Rachel. She was sure that Pete would bring it up at the next Monday night meeting. As a group, they wouldn't interfere with whatever was happening, but they would pay attention just in case they were needed.

Yes, Grace thought to herself as she opened the door, smiling to herself as she smelled the combination of coffee and baking, *something is happening. It won't be long until I discover what it is.*

SIXTEEN

Even though Eddie had said he was taking Connie for a walk around town before going to Bryan's house, he and Connie didn't leave right away. Instead, he turned to watch Grace. He hadn't known her when he was alive, but he had watched her since she and her friends moved to Doveland a few years before.

He liked her. If he had a choice of a grandmother, it would be Grace. His father's mother had not been so kind, or at least he didn't think so since she had rarely seen him. Even as a child, Eddie knew that his father's family had not liked his mother. Families, Eddie snorted to himself. Yes, he was only ten, but he had seen a lot since he had died. He figured he was actually a wise old man by now.

Eddie was rarely in Doveland. He helped anywhere there were people stuck in the in-between. Yes, he lived in the in-between too. But only because he wanted to.

However, recently Eddie had begun to think that perhaps it was time for him to move on. That maybe Connie would be his last case. He had waited for Connie to die, knowing what would happen. Eddie was helping Connie because his mother had asked him to. After this, he could leave.

Eddie glanced over at Connie and wondered what his mother had ever seen in this woman. Connie presented herself as a nothing, but underneath she was equally angry and sad. She probably couldn't figure out which one to be the most, which was one reason she was stuck.

If Eddie didn't know better, he would be angry at Connie for what she had done to his mother. But he knew better. He had seen what anger had done.

Looking around the park, Eddie saw many other people stuck in the in-between. People who didn't know how to leave, or didn't even know they were dead, or didn't accept that they were. But he wasn't there for them. He was there for Connie.

Eddie watched Grace wave at Pete. Yes, they would pay attention. That was a good thing. He had seen how they had helped others in the past few years, and he knew if he had to, he could involve them. For now, it was time to take Connie for a walk around town. It would be interesting to watch what she did with the memories.

• • • ● • ● • ● • • •

At first, Connie hated the idea, and let Eddie know what she thought in no uncertain terms. Walk around the town. For what?

But Eddie ignored her ranting and urged her on until she reluctantly started walking. Walking without actually touching the ground was an odd experience, but after a few blocks, she forgot about the sensation and started paying attention to what she was seeing.

Eddie had told her to let the memories come back to her, not fight them, just pay attention. When she had demanded to know why, he had said that if she ever wanted to leave this in-between place, the only way it would happen was to do what he told her to do. She grudgingly agreed to follow his orders.

As much as Connie didn't want to face anything, she also didn't want to be stuck. When she had asked Eddie where she could go if she weren't stuck, he had told her it was up to her. The way he answered the question sounded ominous. But if it was up to her, she was willing—mostly.

She thought she could probably control the experience so it wouldn't be too bad. After all, she had lived the last part of her life in an in-between place, and survived it.

"Did you?" Eddie asked her.

"Did I what?"

"Survive your self-imposed isolation?" Eddie answered.

"What? Are you reading my mind?"

"How else am I to know what's going on?" Eddie said, walking backward so he could face her. "You've lied to yourself for so long that I can't believe a word you say. At least for now."

Connie stamped her foot—which was very ineffective since it hit nothing—turned, and walked the other way. Eddie let her. He knew that her memories would find her no matter how hard she tried to avoid them.

Walking through the town was just the beginning, and she would find out that was the easiest part.

Without thinking about it, Connie headed towards Edith's family home. Eddie knew she would end up there eventually, so he let her walk alone. Perhaps without him around, she would let herself go back in time and think about what went wrong.

He didn't know exactly what happened. His mother had only told him to help her friend when the time came. She had told him stories of when they were in college together and how Connie had helped her get through school while she hunted for a husband. She had found him his father, Theodore Prince. Not a prince of a man at all.

Eddie knew that one reason his mother had asked him to help Connie was that it would also help him. He needed to know the story, too.

In some ways, Eddie had avoided it the same way that Connie had. But what he did know was that ten years with his father had been enough for him.

SEVENTEEN

Eddie stood in the garden, waiting for Connie to arrive. He had visited the house a few times since he had died, trying to recapture the happiest times of his life.

A few years ago, a new family had moved in that reminded him of what his mother had told him about her family—two kids and loving parents. He wondered what that would have felt like. And watching this family had given him a glimpse into his mother's joyful family life.

When he visited, Eddie would stand in the garden and watch. The garden he remembered had changed through the years, but it was still beautiful. He knew his grandmother would be happy to know that her garden lived on.

Eddie would also go into the house, but only when the family wasn't home. He was always careful not to leave any residual energy behind, just in case someone in the family was what he called "a sensitive." So far, the only beings who had noticed him in all these years were the pets. But they couldn't say anything, so he felt safe visiting.

This was not the house he grew up in. Eddie and his mother and father lived in a much bigger house in Pittsburgh. But he had visited this house with his mother. His father never came with them.

He remembered always wanting to stay. He never wanted to go home. He would beg, cry, pout, argue, but nothing worked. His mother said that she had agreed to be a wife until death parted them, so he and his mother always returned to his father's house.

His grandparents would ask his mother to stay, too. Sometimes they begged her to at least leave Eddie with them. Eddie would stand between Ralph and Lorraine, hugging their legs, praying that his mother would say yes, and he wouldn't have to leave.

But she never changed her mind. His mother would tell them she had made a choice, and it was her duty to stick with it. Eddie was all that she had. She couldn't leave him behind.

All four of them would cry as they said goodbye, and he didn't stop sobbing quietly in the back seat until they reached their house, where he would force himself to stop. He knew his father would punish him if he didn't appear to be happy to come home. And even worse, his father might tell them they couldn't visit again, which would be the most terrible thing he could imagine.

Eddie loved his grandparents, Ralph and Lorraine, and he knew that they loved him. Too much, maybe. Because they had both died within weeks of each other, a year after his death.

When they died, Ralph and Lorraine had not remained in the in-between, so he hadn't seen them since that last visit when they were all alive. Eddie hoped that he could find them once he had finished this task. Maybe they could live together.

But as wise as Eddie had become, he still didn't know exactly how that worked. Eddie hoped that by working with Connie, he would discover how and where to find his grandparents.

Eddie's Uncle Bill had come to their house a few times as he was growing up. Even then, Eddie knew that Bill didn't like his father. The feeling was mutual. And as much as his mother tried to calm the tension between them, it was never a pleasant visit.

Eventually, his Uncle had stopped coming and only sent cards and letters. Eddie knew that he hadn't received them all because sometimes Bill would refer to something he had never heard before.

So Eddie had learned to get to the mail first, before his father. He would read the letter and then destroy it, keeping whatever his Uncle Bill had said locked inside his heart. He didn't even tell his mother, afraid that somehow she would blurt that information out during one of his father's daily interrogations.

He saw his uncle again when he came to his funeral. Bill had cried so hard his shoulders shook. For a moment, Eddie thought Bill had seen him because he glanced up at Eddie when he put his arm around him. But then, shaking his head, Bill had reached for his partner's hand, and they had sat weeping together, their hands hidden beneath the coat that lay between them.

Now that he could make his own choices, being dead and all, Eddie would visit Bill and Terrance once in a while. It made him happy to see how their lives had smoothed out and how they didn't have to hide as much anymore. He knew that Connie had been good friends with his Uncle.

What Eddie didn't know was why Bill and Connie hadn't stayed in touch. It wasn't because of Terrance. His mother had told him that Connie had known about Bill, long before anyone else in the family suspected.

Connie had even tried to tell her about Bill while they were still in college. His mother was ashamed that she hadn't listened, and that she didn't accept it as quickly as Connie had. It was one of her regrets. One of many.

Eddie knew that his mother was counting on him to make right what went wrong. Not him, really, Connie. He would help Connie in the in-between, and Bryan would help in the real world. Or at least the world where people were alive and sometimes acted that way. For Eddie, the in-between was very real.

Watching Connie approach the house, Eddie knew that she was ready. If she could have cried actual tears, that was what she was doing. Sobbing. Yes, she was ready.

Let the fun begin, Eddie said sarcastically to himself.

EIGHTEEN

Bryan and Rachel paused outside of Bryan's house before going in. It was as if they had traveled back in a time machine.

For both of them, it was as if they were in high school again. They both half-expected Bryan's mom to open the door to let them in the way she always did. They would study together or drop off their books and head to the woods. They sighed in unison. Those days were long gone.

Finally, Bryan reached into his pocket and pulled out the key, unlocked the door, and waited for Rachel to step inside. He knew what she would see. A house that looked the same as the last time she had been there for his father's wake. He hadn't had the energy to do anything different.

Besides, if he changed things, he would have to admit that his parents were gone. But seeing the house through Rachel's eyes, he knew that he needed to accept that nothing was the same. His parents had died. But if his mother was telling the truth, they were together. That meant something, didn't it?

He had barely talked to Rachel on the day of his father's funeral. A mumbled hello when she came to the door, and a hasty retreat to the kitchen, using the excuse that his mother needed help, saved him from saying more.

But eventually, he had to come out of the kitchen, still pretending to ignore her while looking at her every chance he got. His mother had urged him to talk to her, knowing how he felt, but he couldn't. He was a failure. She was not. He felt old. She looked the same, at least to him. Rachel had spoken with his mother, hugged her, and left with a nod to Bryan.

Now he stood behind Rachel, wanting her to turn so he could touch her face and tell her how sorry he was for being such a jerk. He could almost hear his mother urging him on, but he still couldn't bring himself to say anything. Instead, he walked past her into the kitchen to make them both a cup of coffee. Rachel headed into the living room and sat on the couch, where she had always sat when they studied together.

Instead of sitting beside her as he used to when they were in high school, Bryan chose the chair facing her, his back against the window knowing that the light behind him would keep her from seeing the emotions that he couldn't keep from moving across his face.

Clearing his throat, he thanked her for helping him.

Rachel practically bounced on the couch in response, making him smile despite his misgivings. She was like a bright yellow canary in a black and white world. She always brought color to his life, to everyone's life, really. It was one of the many reasons both his parents had loved her. They knew she brought him to life. Once again, regret washed over him.

"Are you kidding? This is the most exciting thing to happen to me ever. How will I know when Eddie and Connie get here? Do you think I will ever be able to see them? How did your mother 'open the door' for them? Wait, is your mother here? Can I talk to her?"

Bryan couldn't help laughing. Rachel's enthusiasm always made life better.

"No, I think mom is gone. I only saw her a few times after she died. I miss her, though. It's selfish of me to wish that she had stayed around to help me, but she told me my dad was waiting for her, and she had to go.

"How she opened the door, I don't know. I didn't see her for a few weeks after she died. Then one day, I was lying in bed, and she came in and told me to get up. She scared the crap out of me. I thought I was dreaming. She was real, but she wasn't.

"She reached out to push me like she did when I was a kid, I guess I was always lazy, but it didn't work. That's when I knew that I was crazy or dreaming. I screamed, rolled over, pulled the covers over my head, hoping that whatever was happening would stop.

"When nothing else happened, I turned back to look, and she was gone. But she kept coming back, and I kept turning away until one day I decided to pretend that what was happening was real, and that I hadn't imagined it.

"That's when we started talking, and I accepted that it was my mother. We talked about you, Rachel, how much she liked you. And me, and my life, and what I hadn't done with it. She told me I had a gift, and I needed to accept it."

Bryan put his cup down and dropped his head into his hands. Rachel waited.

When he looked up, he asked, "How can this be a gift? I barely understand what's happening, and I am frightened all the time that I will do it wrong."

Rachel put her cup down, got up, and walked over to Bryan, kneeling, so she was directly in front of him.

"Bryan, you have always worried too much about getting it wrong. And I, for one, am tired of it."

Rachel reached out, put both hands on the side of Bryan's face, and leaned in and kissed him on the lips.

"Now. That's done. It wasn't wrong. You could have done that years ago, and it wouldn't have been wrong."

Rachel stood, walked back to the sofa, sat down, picked up her coffee mug as if nothing had happened, leaned back into the cushions, tucking her legs under her as she always did, and said, "Okay. Tell me more about what your mom told you."

Bryan started to speak, his face still flushed from what happened, when he stopped and said, "They're here."

NINETEEN

Connie took in the house. It reminded her of her own—locked in the past. Eddie had told her that both of Bryan's parents had died, and he hadn't moved on. It looked to her as if he hadn't ever moved at all. The parallel to her own life didn't escape her.

The difference was, she once had a beautiful life, and then ran away from it. To Connie, Bryan looked as if he had never started living. On the other hand, the girl—the woman—on the couch, was like a bright beam of sunshine. It relieved Connie that she wouldn't have to deal with somber Bryan on her own.

Bryan had stood when they arrived and then stood looking like an idiot trying to decide what to do next.

Connie had turned to Eddie and asked him if this was really the person who would help her do whatever she was supposed to be doing so she could move on.

Eddie was already sitting by Rachel, grinning like an idiot, much to Bryan's dismay. He gave her a simple "yep" and then reached over and held Rachel's hand.

Rachel looked down at her hand, wondering why it felt different.

"Don't do that," Bryan said to Eddie.

"Do what?" Rachel said, thinking he was talking to her.

"Oh, this is a mess," Bryan answered, looking from Connie to Eddie.

"Could you both sit together somewhere so I can focus? And is it at all possible to make it so Rachel could see you? Assuming she wants to, of course," he added.

"Yes! I want to! Why did you say, 'don't do that?' Were you talking to me?"

"It's Eddie. He's holding your hand."

Rachel smiled and looked where she thought Eddie might be and said, "Oh, so sweet. Wait, how old is he?"

"Now see, that's the problem. Eddie looks ten, but he's been dead for..."

"Forty years," Connie finished for Bryan. "Don't look so smug, Eddie. Yes, I knew when you died. Yes, I was wrong not to come to your funeral. But how could I?"

Rachel stood and dragged a chair across the room so she could be beside Bryan and said, "I know something is happening, and yes, it's making me crazy, only having a feeling that something is going on. But if Eddie and Connie would sit on the couch, or float, or whatever you do together, at least I can pretend to see you. But, Bryan, you will have to tell me what they are saying. Otherwise, I have no idea how I can help."

Eddie sighed when Rachel had stood and taken her hand away. It had felt so good. She reminded him of his mother—when she was happy—which wasn't often. And Rachel was right. She would not be much help if she couldn't hear and see them.

"Tell her to touch you when we are here, and she'll be able to see and hear us."

After Bryan told her what Eddie said, Rachel tentatively reached out and put her hand on Bryan's arm.

"Oh!" was all she could say. Sitting on the couch was a young boy and an older woman who looked tired, bored, and scared at the same time. The boy was smiling at her, and she couldn't help smiling back.

"Okay," Eddie said. "Now that's done, let's get down to business. Bryan, you have to help Connie change her past."

"I know that," Bryan said. "What I don't know is how I can do that."

Looking toward Rachel, he added, "Or we can do that. Does she go back in time somehow? Like that? Like a ghost? Like a person? And then change what is past? I've read enough books to know that changing the past can be dangerous. That's assuming that it can be done."

"Oh, it can be," Eddie said. "Although it's true, that's not usually a good idea, so it's rarely done. But my mother, Edith," Eddie said, giving Connie a searing look, "made me promise to help this person, and I am keeping my promise, and you are the one that will help me. And her, of course," Eddie said, smiling at Rachel.

Rachel smiled back. She liked this boy.

"Cut it out, you two," Bryan said.

"I agree," Connie chimed in. "Stop it. Be serious. This is my life we are talking about. Eddie, why in the world would your mother want to help me?"

"I don't know, missy," Eddie snipped, still smiling at Rachel. "All she told me is that she couldn't rest easy until you, her best friend, was free."

"Free? Free from what?" Connie snapped back.

But even as she did so, she knew what her friend had meant. She hadn't been free since that day she had made the fateful decision that brought both her and her daughter, Karla, into a life barely lived.

"Yes, that," Eddie said, turning to look directly at Connie.

"She wants you to be free of the in-between. She wants you to have lived the life you were meant to live, not the one you hid away in."

While Connie glared at Eddie, Rachel looked back and forth between them and finally said, "Okay, here's what I don't understand, well there is a lot I don't understand. But let's start with this.

"If Connie made a mistake that changed her life, how long ago was it? No matter when it was, how can we go back in time to help her? If there is such a thing. We either wouldn't be born yet, or we would be like ghosts like her or something..." Rachel trailed off, thinking about how illogical it all sounded.

Eddie stood and started pacing the room. Now that Rachel could see him, as long as she remembered to keep her hand on Bryan's arm, it didn't matter that he wasn't staying still.

"Okay, let me try to explain how the past might be changed. Think of it as a game of spider. You know the card game people play on their phones?"

Bryan started laughing.

"Time is like the game of spider? Are you serious?"

Eddie glared at Bryan, "What do you know? You, like Connie here, decided to not live in the time you have had, learned nothing new, didn't stretch out into the world and use your imagination about what you could do, or how you could be of service. Instead, you both ran away."

Turning to Rachel, Eddie said, "And you. You waited for this idiot to come to his senses. Would he ever if his mommy hadn't come back to help him?

"Life on earth is a gift. One to be lived. And yes, I can use the spider game to explain how you could change the past if you will attempt to try."

TWENTY

As Eddie launched into his explanation of how life and time were like the game of spider, the three people who were listening got a glimpse of what he meant.

Rachel had often played the game, but Connie and Bryan had not. So as Eddie talked, Rachel nodded her head, while the other two tried to follow the logic of what he was saying.

Eddie explained that spider is a card game. The player tries to line up the cards into a run, starting with the king and ending with the ace. Once that happens, that group of cards is removed from the deck.

The game begins with a row of cards with the top card facing up. The rest of the deck sits on the side, ready to be used. The player moves the cards around, aiming for a run, but when there aren't any more moves, a new row of cards are dealt from the stack waiting on the side. This continues until all the cards have lined up and are removed from the deck.

But of course, sometimes the player gets stuck at the end, and there were no more chances to line up the cards.

Eddie explained that if you play the game in an app on your phone or computer, you can correct your mistakes. You can go back a few moves. You can even go back to the beginning. Every time you go back, you can notice what you had tried before and try different combinations until one of them works.

Instead of claiming failure because the cards didn't line up correctly, one can try over and over again until everything lines up and then complete the game.

As Eddie finished his explanation, Rachel added, "That's assuming that you have a winning hand, which you can choose to be dealt in the app's setting."

She paused a moment and added, "So in this analogy, you are saying that life is like a game, a winning game, and that you can correct mistakes until you get it right?"

"Essentially," Eddie answered. "Unless people give up." Eddie stared at both Connie and Bryan.

"And don't have the courage to keep correcting what they are doing in life. Then it's their fault. Because everyone has a winning hand."

"Eddie, I don't think it helps to make Bryan and Connie feel bad about their choices. And in some ways, you would have to include me since I have been waiting for this idiot, as you put it."

Rachel smiled at Bryan as she called him an idiot, so he would know what she meant.

"Humans get afraid, Eddie. I know you know that."

"Okay, I'll leave out the blaming stuff."

Eddie and Rachel smiled at each other, and Bryan tried, and failed, not to feel jealous. He knew it was stupid to be jealous of a boy who had died forty years before, but it was hard not to.

Rachel and Eddie were like two best buds without even knowing each other. He had known Rachel his entire life and didn't have that kind of connection.

The irony, or maybe perfection, of what was happening hit him as Eddie smiled at him, too.

"Oh," Bryan said, "This is not just about Connie. This is about me. And Rachel!"

Eddie started to say, "Give this man a star," when he remembered what Rachel had asked of him, so he more politely answered with a simple, "yes."

Rachel looked at Eddie, Connie, and Bryan, wondering what had brought them all together, and then had a thought. "Wait. This is happening because your mothers knew each other, isn't it?"

"Keep this one," Eddie said to Bryan.

"Yes, my mother and Bryan's mother, Jillyan, went to school together. The two of them decided that these two—Connie and Bryan—needed a chance to live."

Hearing Rachel catch her breath, he added, "No, Bryan is not going to die—at least not that I know about—they meant for him to start living."

"When did they decide this? Before they died, or after?"

"After. In the in-between. So when I told you that my mom asked me to help Connie, it was your mother too, Bryan. It was the two of them who came up with this plan. If they helped you discover your gift of seeing people in the in-between, and learned how to help them, you would find meaning in your life, and my mother will have helped right what she felt had gone wrong in Connie's life."

No one said anything. Rachel looked back and forth between the three of them. Bryan looked as if someone had slapped him across the face and handed him a Christmas present at the same time. Connie looked like a white statue. Unmoving. Eddie had sat back on the couch, looking like a young boy and a middle-aged man in one package.

She had so many questions for Eddie. What was the in-between? Did everyone go there at first? Why? Where did the people go after they left? Did people stay there by choice, or were they stuck? Was he still there because he promised his mother, or was there another reason too? What did he get out of it?

And since it now involved her, what did she get out of it? Was this about her and Bryan, or was there more?

"So many questions," Eddie said in a tired voice. Leaning back against the old couch in a t-shirt that said, "Don't worry, be happy," Eddie looked exhausted.

No wonder, Rachel thought. He is trying to bring us all into something we didn't know existed. It must be tiring.

When she heard the words, "It is," in her head, she looked at Eddie, and he winked.

Rachel realized that she shouldn't be surprised. He probably knew what everyone was thinking. After all, he was what people called a ghost. But then, so was Connie.

Rachel spoke, "Not sure what my role in all this is, but I have more questions. I think I see what you mean about the spider game, Eddie. Connie can go back to someplace in time—somehow, since I still don't know that part—and do something different from what she did before, until what went wrong comes out right."

'Basically," Eddie answered.

"Well, if that's true," Rachel said, turning to Connie, "What went wrong?"

TWENTY ONE

Connie didn't answer, not moving. If possible, she had gotten paler. With her eyes closed, Connie looked lifeless. Which Rachel realized was the point. She was lifeless, and if Eddie was telling the truth, she had been lifeless even before she died.

Outside the window, Rachel could hear chickadees calling to each other. She knew that Bryan's mom, Jillyan, had been a lover of birds and gardens, and Bryan had kept up that part of the house, at least.

"They had that in common," Eddie said. "My mother and Jillyan loved birds and gardens. But we moved away, and mom wasn't allowed to garden at my father's house. The gardener did it. 'We don't get our hands dirty,' my father's mother would say to my mom.

"It was another reason mom loved coming home to visit her parents. As soon as we arrived, she would grab her gloves and head out to dig in the dirt with her mother."

Eddie walked over to Connie and directed his next words to her with a force that surprised even Rachel.

"You remember that, don't you, Connie? Mom told me about you as she worked in the garden. She told me about her friend from college. The friend who was like a sister to her and her brother, and another daughter to her parents. It's the one thing you kept—the love of birds and gardens.

"Did you think of my mother when you were out there working in your garden, pretending to live? Or had you forgotten her just like you forgot everything else about the life you had promised my grandparents and the women in the trailer park that you would live?

"Did you forget all of them? Did you do it out of spite? Or was it a mistake?"

When Connie still didn't move, Eddie reached out and slapped her face. The slap was a surprise, but so was the fact that Eddie actually connected with her face.

Connie reached up and held her hand to her face, looked at Eddie, and said, "You already know I didn't do it on purpose. I was afraid. I made the wrong choice. I made a mistake."

Eddie backed away and stared at her. It was strange to watch a young boy confront a woman who could be his grandmother, but then Rachel knew that Eddie had long ago grown into a wise man, no matter what his form looked like now.

"People make mistakes all the time, Connie. All. The. Time. Your mistake was not facing up to it, which surprises me. Mom told me about how when you were young you defied people to become someone. Why not do it then? Are you willing to stand up to it now?"

"Yes. I am willing. But I don't understand how. Assuming that I can go back in time, do I stop what happened, or what I did afterward?"

Bryan had sat quietly, observing the group. It was so different from walking in the woods. He understood the creatures there. People confused him. It was only because it was his mother that he was willing.

And the fact that Eddie was right. He had been a coward. It was time for him to live, and he was going to do it by helping two dead people.

"Why not tell us the story, Connie? Then perhaps we can help you decide how far back to go. And I will be able to figure out my part in this."

"And mine," Rachel added.

Bryan turned to Rachel and corrected himself, "Our part in this."

• • • ● • ● • ● • • •

As Grace poured coffee and served pastries, her mind drifted to what she had overheard that morning. She had to admit that it made her excited and curious. She was ready to be part of something new again.

The past year had been quiet, at least compared to previous years. When they had all moved to Doveland, they had stirred up trouble without meaning to. There had been so many secrets uncovered, she and her friends often held daily meetings to discuss what to do.

Now it was too quiet. Grace understood that the door to the Erda dimension had been closed, so there were no more visits between the two dimensions of Earth and Erda.

Her husband, Eric, had returned from Erda, and passed away soon after that, having forgotten everything about his brief time in Erda. He had returned to be with her, thinking his illness was cured. Later, when he discovered that it wasn't gone, Eric assured Grace he didn't care. He would rather spend a day with her, then years without her.

Grace wiped a tear from her eyes. She had been alone before Eric, and although she was alone again, it was not the same. Now, Grace knew that everything she saw or experienced with her five senses was not all there was to the world.

Now she knew that there were other dimensions and other spaces in the universe. She had learned that people didn't die. They simply moved somewhere else.

Before Eric died, she had released him.

"Don't stay here for me," she had said, "I'll find you later wherever you go, just as we found each other here."

He had smiled, and his eyes had said thank you to her. That first night after his passing, Eric had stood at the foot of her bed and told her again that he loved her. Then he was gone. And she had never seen him again, which was what she wanted for him.

She meant it when she told him they would find each other again. Because now she knew that's how it worked. People always found each other again if they had agreed to it.

So when she saw Jillyan's boy, Bryan, apparently speaking to no one, Grace knew he wasn't talking to the air. Someone was there. Grace knew the woman with him too, or at least she had seen her around town.

Thinking about Pete's nod to her through the window, she thought that maybe they shouldn't wait until Monday night to get together.

Something was niggling at her, and Grace knew, after years of paying attention to niggling, that ignoring that little voice that told her that something was happening was never a good idea.

TWENTY TWO

Connie looked around the room and wondered how she had ever gotten to this place. Dead and only three people to talk to. There was no one to blame but herself. So, if it were possible to change the past, she would try.

"Are you sending me back now?" Connie asked.

Eddie looked at her with his clear blue eyes that reminded Connie so much of his mother.

"No. First, you will tell us what you think happened. Play out the game so we can see what you did."

"Where do I start?"

"Before the wedding," Eddie replied.

Connie closed her eyes and drifted back to that time, seeing it as it was happening all over again.

That spring break, when Edith announced her engagement, Edith was radiant. Her happiness spread throughout the family. It was impossible not to be happy for her. Theodore Prince was her dream come true. Handsome, charming, and rich enough to take care of her and the family she wanted to have.

Connie's trepidation about Theo was something that she kept to herself. She told herself that she was only worried because Theo offered Edith a life that she would find stifling. She also had to admit that a part of her was jealous. But Connie didn't let any of that show. Instead, she did all the things that a maid of honor should do for the bride.

The two of them went to lunch and giggled over the plans. Lorraine joined them as they thumbed through bridal magazines, looking for ideas that they could afford. Although Ralph made a good living, they weren't wealthy enough to provide everything that Edith wanted. It didn't matter. They were enjoying the dreaming.

Then Theo's mother, Virginia, stepped in. After hearing about the plans for a wedding in a small chapel in Doveland, she said it wasn't big enough. Seeing the dress Edith had planned to wear, Virginia said it wasn't good enough, and bought her another dress. Invitations to family and friends were changed to include people that even Theo hadn't heard of before.

Connie and Virginia disliked each other at first sight. Connie kept her feelings to herself, Virginia did not. She did everything she could to derail Connie's place at Edith's wedding. Virginia changed the colors and style of the bridesmaid dresses to ones that didn't look good on Connie.

When Connie's name came up, Virginia would lift her head just enough, so she was looking down her nose at what they were talking about. She called Connie trailer trash behind her back, but loud enough that Connie would hear.

There was nothing that Connie could do. She did come from a trailer park. She did have a drunk, abusive, loud-mouthed, uneducated father and an absent mother. Her friends growing up were the women of the trailer park. If that made someone trailer trash, then yes, that was what she was. So she took it, not refuting Virginia's innuendos and her direct insults.

Edith's family didn't fare much better. Virginia constantly overturned Lorraine's choices for her daughter's wedding. Virginia questioned Ralph's' business acumen, insinuating that he was incompetent. And Bill. They didn't even mention his name. It was as if Bill didn't exist.

Theo's dad, Joseph, stayed in the background, ignoring his wife and the family that would soon join them. But when Joseph was present, he was like an older version of his son—handsome and charming and vaguely sinister.

Connie couldn't decide which member of the Prince family that she disliked the most. But for the sake of her friend, she kept those thoughts to herself.

Although Edith cried more than once after Virginia overruled her choices for the wedding, Theo would soothe and comfort her, and she would smile through her tears and agree that it was all for the best.

After all, they had to make a good impression on all the Prince's friends, family, and business acquaintances. These were the people who would be the source that would provide for the stable family life she wanted.

As Connie told the story of the months of preparation for Edith's wedding, she glanced over at Eddie. How did he feel about hearing about the past? But he gave her a blank look and a hand gesture that meant to continue. So she did.

She and Edith finished up their last few months of school differently. Their small apartment off-campus was always busy with friends visiting and Friday night parties. Bridal magazines, mixed with business journals, sat on their coffee table.

Connie had splurged and gotten an electric typewriter, and she was on it all the time writing letters to companies, and following up with the interviews she had with the recruiters who came to the school.

Although they weren't looking for women, she was so impressive that many were considering hiring her. Ralph had written her a glowing letter of recommendation, which helped tremendously.

Finally, right before school ended, she chose the company. It had an office in Pittsburgh, which meant she wouldn't be that far from Ralph and Lorraine, or even the trailer park if she decided to visit.

Edith would be in Pittsburgh too, but Connie knew that Theo would discourage Edith from inviting her to their house. However, she figured that she and Edith would meet in Doveland whenever they wanted to see each other.

Connie paused and looked around the room. Eddie kept his blank look, not giving away anything. Bryan looked bored. Only Rachel appeared interested.

When no one said anything, Rachel was the one who asked, "Did the wedding go well?"

"If big weddings made to impress are your thing, then yes."

Eddie cleared his throat.

"I've heard enough for now. I think what needs to happen before Connie can go back in time is she needs to practice changing things right now. You know, act like a friend. Help people."

"Like what? How?"

"Go out there and find people that need help and then help them."

"But I'm dead."

"That's what makes this job easy," Eddie said. "You need to practice becoming alive enough to change something for the better."

"Oh!" Rachel said, "She'll do things like an angel."

"Exactly," Eddie said.

"Are you kidding me?" Connie snapped. "I'm no angel."

"Well, that's true," Eddie said with the tiniest sneer. "But you can learn to be one. I'm going to help you with this first one."

Turning to Bryan and Rachel, he added, "We'll find you two later."

With that, they were gone.

TWENTY THREE

The next thing Connie knew, she and Eddie were hanging in the air, watching cars and trucks fly by on a freeway far below them. They were so far above them they looked like the Hot-Wheel toy cars she had seen children play with.

After adjusting to the view, and the fact she was so high up but it didn't feel any different from being on the ground, Connie asked, "What are we doing here?"

"Watch. In a minute, something will begin to happen that you can stop. Let's see if you can do it."

Connie asked how she would know, and how she would stop it, but instead of answering Eddie just smiled.

A split second later, Connie was standing beside the freeway. The rush of the cars and trucks speeding by was overwhelming. Even though she was already dead, it terrified Connie. Eddie had done his vanishing act, and she had no idea what she was supposed to do next.

With nowhere to go and nothing else to do, Connie started watching the drivers as they rushed past her. The more she watched, the clearer her vision of each driver was to her as they sped by. It was as if each one was still for a moment, like a pause button on a recording.

It was amazing how many things were going on in each vehicle. One woman was actually putting on makeup while speeding by in her car.

A mother was yelling at the kids in the back seat to be quiet. A man smoked, his hand hanging out the side of the car, letting the smoke drift away.

People sang along to the songs playing in their cars. A few seemed to be practicing with language tapes. Connie heard a snatch of her favorite NPR show and realized that it meant it was Saturday. Then she remembered that people listened to recordings of things like that, which meant it could be any day of the week.

For a moment, Connie felt even more disoriented, if that were possible. She not only didn't know what day of the week it was, but she also didn't know what month it was. How long had she been dead? And where was she? She didn't recognize the freeway or the surrounding areas. Nothing was familiar. Without thinking, she turned around and stepped back—directly into the path of a semi-trailer.

Connie screamed. The driver kept going as if nothing had happened. After recovering from the shock and returning to the side of the road, Connie asked herself if nothing could hurt her now. She found herself pleased with that thought. It was as if she had gained a superpower. The pleasure faded when she remembered that she couldn't do anything with it.

Or could she? Maybe she could. Perhaps that was why she was there. After all, Eddie told her to help, which meant she could. Why else was she there? Why would Eddie put her beside a freeway, if he didn't want her to do anything? So what could she do? What did Eddie want her to do? Help someone? How?

Connie turned her attention back to the drivers. She figured that was what she was supposed to do had something to do with what was happening, or going to happen, right where she was standing.

Eddie might think she was stupid, and perhaps she had been. But she hadn't always been such a loser, and Eddie was definitely not stupid. He was counting on her to figure it out. Whoever needed help was also counting on her to figure it out, even if they didn't know that. Yet.

As a blue car came towards her, Connie caught sight of a face staring out of the back window. A small child, strapped into a car seat, looked right at her and waved.

Without thinking, Connie waved back, and the child smiled at her and waved harder.

Connie laughed out loud. She had been seen!

• • • • • • • • • •

Angie Harris played with the radio dial. She needed something to listen to, something to take her mind off what had just happened.

Angie had yelled at her boss, and he had fired her. How was she going to take care of her son if she didn't have a job? Tears streamed down her face, and she brushed them away, angry at herself for feeling sad, for being afraid, and most of all, for yelling at that horrid man.

Yes, he was horrid. Yes, Angie hated her job. Yes, he deserved her anger, but none of that mattered. What mattered is she had barely enough money to pay the babysitter. The car was so old it rattled while she drove. And now the radio didn't work. She smacked it, hoping that whatever was wrong with it would be fixed with a good whack.

That's what her father used to say as he would haul off and hit her and her brother. He would fix them with a good whack.

She had learned to be quiet, never to say anything about her feelings. Yes, she had learned that, so why hadn't she stayed quiet today? Fresh tears poured down her face, blurring her vision.

The car sputtered. Fear spiked throughout her body.

"Oh, no. Not here!"

She was on the slow lane of the freeway, but there was nowhere to pull off. Cars and trucks were behind her, going as fast as they could. She would die. Her son would be without a mother. The people in the cars behind her would be injured. All because she was poor and couldn't fix her car.

"Please, God,' Angie yelled, "Help me!"

The car sputtered once more and then stopped. Connie shut her eyes, waiting for the inevitable crash. Hoping it was painless.

A moment passed.

Then someone tapped on her window.

Startled, Angie looked up to see a man in a business suit tapping on her window. She rolled it down, wondering if she was dead, and God had granted her wish that her death would be painless.

"Am I dead?" Angie asked the man with kind, dark eyes.

He didn't laugh. Instead, he said, "I saw you pull off, and thought you might need some help."

Only then did Angie see that somehow she was now safely parked on the side of the road. Something made her look in her rearview mirror, and for a moment, she saw a woman standing behind her, smiling. When she looked again, the woman was gone, but the man was still there.

Stepping out of her car, she took his hand. And at that moment, Angie knew that she and her son would be fine from now on.

"Thank you," she whispered, now knowing that someone was listening to her, and she and her life mattered.

TWENTY FOUR

Connie was still smiling when she appeared again in Bryan's living room. For Rachel and Bryan, nothing had changed. But for Connie, it was a whole new world. A child had waved at her. An accident had been averted. And hope had come to a woman who had thought she had nothing.

Turning to Eddie, she asked, "Can I help her more?"

Eddie, for once, smiled back at Connie.

"No need. Others will help her when she needs it."

"The man?"

When Eddie nodded, Connie smiled again.

"Something happened?" Rachel asked.

With the slightest hint of pride in his voice, Eddie answered, "Connie passed her first test."

Connie continued smiling as Eddie told the story of what happened. Only when he finished did she ask the question she had been burning to ask since the moment she saw the car parked on the side of the freeway.

"How did I do that? I don't know how it happened. I just wanted her to be safe, and then she was. How can I do it again if I don't know what I did? And what if I would have failed? Would she have died?"

Eddie sighed before answering.

"You had backup, just in case. And the more you do this, the more control you will have of what you are doing. That's a good thing, because when you go back in time, everything will be much more difficult."

Turning to Bryan, he added, "Bryan, you will watch over her. First from here as she practices, and then when she returns to the past."

When everyone started talking at once, Eddie raised his hand.

"One thing at a time. Bryan will be Connie's guide. Since he is not dead, he will communicate with her through the door his mother opened for him. Rachel, you are his anchor. With you here, he can follow the line back to you so he won't get lost in the in-between with Connie."

Rachel and Bryan turned to look at each, and Rachel's hand tightened on Bryan's arm.

Eddie ignored them and continued, "It will work the same way when we go into the past. But for now, the three of you need some practice working this out together."

"Wait," Bryan said, "I don't understand why it has to be me. Aren't you her guide? Why can't you do this with her?"

Eddie raised his hands in frustration. If he hadn't promised his mother and Bryan's mother to help these two, he would just leave now. He was tired of these people already.

The truth was, he was just tired of it all. He was tired of having to train people to be helpers in the in-between. Sometimes they already knew that they were, but didn't know how to help effectively. Other times it was a slog waking them up to what they were there to do.

Once in a while, he had met people that taught him something or were delightful to be around, but mostly, he was teaching the unenlightened and often the unwilling.

Jillyan had promised Eddie that her son Bryan would be willing, just to give him a chance. That's what Eddie was doing, or trying to do.

Because of his promise, and despite his irritations with everyone, Eddie answered Bryan as politely as possible.

"Bryan, this is a gift. Like all gifts, it can feel like a burden sometimes. Trust me. I know this. But if you don't accept this gift and make the most of it, you'll live a life without meaning and purpose, just as you have been doing up to now. You might be alive, but your life will be dead. Is that what you want?

"Besides, I won't always be here. I am leaving after this is over. But there will be others who will come to you, and you will help them.

"What you don't know, Bryan, is that there have always been people who have come to you, but you ignored them because you had that door to that awareness fully closed. You, my friend, were almost as dead as Connie here."

Sighing again, and running his hands through his hair, Eddie said, "I'm tired. I need to rest. You do, too. Go home, Rachel. Go away, Connie. Bryan, get some rest. Tomorrow we'll begin again."

Before Eddie had finished speaking, he had begun to fade out. Watching him go, Connie did the same. She wanted to go back to Edith's house and sit in the garden and watch the birds.

When both of them were gone, Rachel turned to Bryan, kissed him on the cheek, and let herself out the front door. Rachel had so many questions but didn't know where to direct them. Bryan wouldn't know the answers.

She needed to think.

Why had she understood what Eddie had said? Why wasn't she questioning the truth of what he was saying? Was it because she already knew about this other place? Eddie called it the in-between?

She supposed it was called many different things. The afterlife, maybe? It didn't matter. What mattered was that she was asked to help. And she wanted to. And she believed Eddie. And she and Bryan would work together. She wasn't sure which of those things pleased her the most.

However, Rachel knew that if she would be Bryan's anchor, she needed support, too. What she had to do was not something she could do on her own. But who could she talk to about this? Most people would think she was making it up.

Sure, people loved to hear angel stories, and what Connie had done would definitely be turned into an angel story in that woman's mind.

But Rachel knew that was the extent that most people would be willing to go. There were angels. Understanding how the angel thing worked wasn't necessary to them, just the idea that angels existed was enough.

But for Rachel, just knowing that things existed was never enough. She always wanted to know more. Even though she had needed to put her hand on Bryan's arm to see Connie and Eddie, she had once seen two people on her own. Perhaps that's why she wanted to be part of this so much.

Without thinking about it, Rachel headed to the coffee shop. A nice cup of coffee and one of Grace's pastries would help her think. Maybe she would pick up a book while she was there.

Rachel thought Grace was smart to add books to the coffee shop. It made it so inviting. But Rachel knew it was more than coffee and books that was taking her to Your Second Home.

Grace was the town's busybody. She knew everybody and everything going on in Doveland. Maybe she would help.

TWENTY FIVE

Connie had meant to go to Edith's old house and sit in the garden.

Instead, she found herself waiting outside Bryan's house until Rachel left, and then without thinking about it, she followed her.

She watched as Rachel opened the door to Your Second Home and wave to the woman Connie had seen in the park serving people coffee.

For a moment, Connie hesitated and then took a deep breath and walked through the window into the room. She felt nothing. It was strangely exhilarating. *Being dead might not be that terrible, after all.*

Although the older woman glanced her way as she slid inside, Connie was sure that she hadn't seen her. Connie waited until Rachel found a seat and then stood behind her.

But when that same woman headed to Rachel's table with a coffeepot and glanced her way again, Connie decided that perhaps it was best she stood behind one of the bookcases. Maybe some people didn't see her, but they felt her presence.

Rachel glanced up as Grace stood at the table looking behind her and then turning back to Rachel, took her order.

"Thanks, Grace," Rachel said.

Ah, Connie thought, *now I know her name.*

A few minutes later, Grace returned to the table, bringing Rachel's order, and then asked if Rachel would mind if she sat with her. Rachel smiled at Grace, thinking how wise this woman must be. Grace must know that she needed to talk to someone.

The two of them chatted about things around town for a bit, and then Grace mentioned that she had seen Rachel with Bryan in the park. Rachel leaned back in her chair and looked at the woman sitting across from her.

Grace's brown eyes were alert and kind. A pair of glasses hung from a chain around her neck. Her steel gray hair was styled in a fluffy cut framing her slightly plump face. Rachel thought Grace was the picture of what grandmothers looked like in books. Except Rachel knew Grace didn't have any children. That much gossip had circled the town when Grace and her friends had first arrived.

Rachel glanced around the coffee shop. There was no one there but them. A rare occurrence. Perhaps this was meant to be.

"You have questions, dear?" Grace prompted.

Rachel nodded.

"But I don't know where to start. I have heard rumors about you and some of your friends. That you do 'magical' things, know things others don't, do things that others can't do. Are the rumors true?"

Grace smiled at Rachel before answering.

"Oh, not me. I am just someone who pays attention. But yes, I have friends that some people might call 'magical,' but really, it's just different gifts. Some people have them and don't know that they do, or choose to ignore them. But my friends are aware of them."

"And help others?" Rachel asked.

Behind the bookshelf, Connie started trembling.

Grace smiled, "Yes, and help others. Some of those friends have moved away. My partner in this coffee shop, Mandy, and her husband, Tom, moved away, as did Tom's sister Mira after she married Sam. They come back to visit from time to time."

Grace paused before continuing. "Some of them have gone to another place, and won't be returning."

"What other place?" Rachel asked.

Grace looked at Rachel and wondered how much she needed to tell her, or what Rachel would accept. Would she understand the idea of other dimensions? Would she accept it? Perhaps not.

Trying to explain that they went to another dimension called Erda might be too much. Some people understood and accepted that other planes of existence were real, but not everyone.

For a moment, Grace allowed herself to remember when they had all lived in Doveland.

Then her husband Eric, knowing he was ill, had left with Sarah and Leif because they assured him he would be well in Erda. Eric hadn't stayed there. He missed Grace too much. He had told her that even if he wasn't cured, he would rather spend his last days with her.

Although Eric lost his memory of his time in Erda, he did remember that Suzanne told him she was closing the door between the two dimensions of Earth and Erda because it was safer that way. Sarah, Leif, Suzanne, and Hannah were gone forever.

Grace didn't know what had happened to them. All she knew was that Erda was where they needed to be.

Grace smiled to herself. Those were magnificent days. And although she was often lonely, Grace knew that one day they would all be reunited.

So, there were not that many of them left in town now. But there were enough to help Rachel with whatever was bothering her.

"Why don't you tell me what you need," Grace said as she reached over and laid her hand on top of Rachel's. "I'm sure we can help. We can at least be sympathetic listeners."

Just as Rachel started to say something, a group of people piled into the coffee shop, and the moment passed. Grace knew the group. They were members of the town council. They often stopped by after their meetings were over. One woman caught Grace's eye and smiled at her. Grace waved her over to the table.

"Valerie, do you know Rachel?" Grace asked.

"I've seen you around town," Valerie replied, shaking Rachel's hand.

"Rachel needs a little help. Perhaps we can get the group together tonight and listen to what she needs?"

Valerie looked at Rachel and then back to Grace. "Of course. Shall I pass the word? Do you want everyone? Johnny is in town. Do you want him to come too?"

When Grace nodded yes, Valerie smiled at the two of them and then headed back to the table where the members of the town council waited for her, still smiling. It had been a while since they had an adventure together, and seeing the look in Grace's eyes told Valerie that was exactly what they were heading for.

It would be good for Ava. Although she and her husband, Evan, accepted that their daughter, Hannah, had returned to Erda, it had been hard for them. Helping Rachel might ease the sting of missing her. And Grace. It would help Grace, too. She had handled Eric's death as well as could be expected. But the sparkle of curiosity in her eyes had been absent, and today it had returned.

TWENTY SIX

Eddie found Connie sitting on the park bench, watching the people of Doveland.

When Connie had visited Edith in Doveland, the two of them would often do the same thing. Sit on the park bench and watch the town walk by.

Although some things were new, like the gazebo and Grace's coffee shop, much of it had stayed the same.

Connie was playing a game with herself, wondering what would have happened if she hadn't done what she had done. Would she have continued working and then retired and moved here to Doveland?

Perhaps she would have been friends with that woman, Grace. Maybe there would have been other people she could have laughed with and counted on. Instead, she had run away with her daughter Karla.

Connie tried not to think about Karla. It made her heart hurt. She and Karla had barely made it through Karla's teen years before Karla had left to go to college as far away from her mother as possible. Watching the people of Doveland walk through the park holding hands with their children brought back all the memories, both happy and terrible.

She had taken the wrong path. It was apparent now. Why couldn't it have been evident to her before? Mama Woo had tried to tell her, but she hadn't listened.

Now Edith's son was trying to help her. Connie promised herself that this time she would listen. She hoped it wasn't too late.

That was the mood she was in when Eddie appeared beside her on the bench. The whole time she had been sitting there, no one had seen her, which was both good and bad.

She could watch without being seen, but she was also lonely. Eddie's appearance was welcome. He was someone to talk to and hopefully he was bringing something for her to do. She had sat too long in her life doing nothing important. Now, she felt hungry for a purpose.

Eddie didn't waste any time.

"Are you ready?" he asked, but didn't wait for an answer. A timeless moment later, the two of them were walking down what appeared to be a city street. When she made a motion to ask where they were, Eddie held up his hand.

"It doesn't matter where we are. It matters what you will do here. Can you feel it?"

Connie stopped walking. Listened. Waited for something, anything. If she had decided to listen to Eddie, she would have to trust him too. There was a reason they were here. What was it?

A few minutes passed before Connie saw a girl and a boy walking down the sidewalk holding hands.

Young love, she thought to herself. The girl reminded her of her daughter, Karla, when Karla was that age. She glanced at Eddie, and he nodded. Yes, it had something to do with the two of them.

As she watched, Connie felt something dark coming towards them. Without thinking about it, Connie started running towards the couple. The darkness was moving closer. As she ran, Connie glanced over her shoulder and saw a truck turn the corner and head down the street towards them, moving too fast.

The couple had stopped near a telephone pole. The boy backed up against the pole, pulling the girl closer to him. Neither of them could see the truck from where they stood.

Besides, they were on the sidewalk, and the truck was in the street. But Connie knew. She didn't know how she knew, but she did. The truck was heading straight for them.

She yelled, "Move!" and reaching the couple pushed both of them out of the way. A second later, the truck struck the pole.

As soon as she saw that they were safe, Connie turned back to Eddie with tears in her eyes. Real tears.

"What's happening?" Connie whispered.

A flash later and they were back on the park bench. Connie leaned forward, head in her hands, and tried to catch her breath.

This was new. She could feel the seat a little, she could feel her head in her hands, and the tears that had begun after the near accident continued to flow down her cheeks.

"What's happening?" she asked again.

"You are passing tests. Each time you do, you get closer to being able to return to the past."

Connie stared at Eddie, taking in what he had said. "Are you telling me I am not going back as a ghost when I go back in the past? I'm going back as an actual person?"

When Eddie nodded, smiling in approval at her dawning awareness, she got up from the bench and started walking.

Eddie followed her, even though he was reasonably sure he knew where she was going. Back to his grandparent's house. To sit in the garden.

• • • • • • • • • •

Grace often stood at the window of Your Second Home and stared at the park bench. It was her favorite place to sit. Sometimes when she sat there, she would think about the man who had passed away one night on that bench. She would think about the things she and the town had learned after he died while tracking down who he was and why he had been there.

There was something about the bench that made everyone want to sit on it. But for the last few hours, no one had sat there. They would glance at it and then walk away. It was as if someone was already sitting there, which Grace was sure was happening.

Not that she could see anyone there, but ever since Eric had died, she had felt people around her. It was an interesting experience. Not one that she was sure that she liked. But here it was, and she would embrace it as if it were a gift. She had always tried to say yes to gifts that expanded her world.

After all, it was saying yes to her friend Sarah that had brought her to Doveland. Now Doveland was her home. And the people were her people, including the ones she couldn't see—like whoever was on the bench.

Grace turned away from the window and looked back at the space. She loved it. It was just what she had always wanted. A place people could meet and talk or read—a safe space. Mandy had helped her build it, but now that she and Tom had moved away, Grace had hired people to do most of the work. That meant she could come and go at will.

She waved at the young woman working behind the counter and pointed upstairs. She would know that Grace meant she was heading to her apartment above the store.

If there was an emergency, she could be downstairs in a flash. But if she was having people over that night, she needed to get ready. It had been a while since they had met for something like this.

Yes, Grace thought, this will be exciting.

Before heading upstairs, Grace glanced outside at the bench and saw a mom and her daughter sitting on it.

Whoever had been there must have gone, she thought. And then she wondered if whoever had been there was a part of what was going on with Rachel.

TWENTY SEVEN

While Rachel met with Grace, Bryan returned to the woods. He could walk out the back door of his parent's home, cross the backyard filled with flowers, bushes, and his mother's favorite redbud tree, open the hidden back gate, and within a few feet, he would be in the woods. He didn't know who owned the woods. It had always been there and had always been his escape.

But this time he wasn't escaping from life, he was fleeing from what Eddie had said. Except Bryan knew there was no escape from that, and as he walked, Bryan realized that perhaps he didn't want to escape it, anyway.

What if what Eddie had said about this always being his calling was true? Maybe if he did this thing—as if he had a choice—he would start living.

Bryan understood what Eddie meant. Here he was forty years old, and his life hadn't begun yet. How ironic it would be that it would start by helping those that had died.

Bryan had no trouble understanding that life continued. He saw it every day in the woods. The system lived because the pieces of it appeared to die and then live again in another way. Which for Bryan meant that life always went on. Life could not include death.

Although Bryan knew that most people thought of death as the end of life, that wasn't possible. As he had reasoned for himself long ago, if there was death in life, death would eventually eliminate everything. Since that didn't happen, and he had witnessed the cycle of life in the woods year after year, Bryan knew that life was a forever thing. How that worked, Bryan didn't know. That wasn't the important part. That it was true, that was what was essential.

Knowing that life continued had helped him when his dad and mom died. It was what his mother must have meant when she told him he had just refused to see the open door, so she showed it to him. Bryan wondered about all the things that his mother must have known, and that he hadn't asked her about.

Like never asking her about Edith. Although he had known she once had a friend named Edith, he couldn't remember what happened to her.

Obviously, Edith had a son. Had his mother mentioned him, and he ignored her? How had Eddie died? Where was the father? What had Connie done that kept her stuck in the in-between? If they didn't succeed, what would happen to her? To him? To Rachel? Was this going to be a safe thing to do?

A red-tailed hawk startled Bryan as it swooped through the trees, coming within feet of him, screaming as it did so. Then, soaring through the trees, it flew higher until Bryan could see it in the clear blue sky through the tree canopy opening.

"Okay, I get it," Bryan said to the hawk. "It's not about being safe. It's about being who I am."

Bryan chose to believe that the hawk had gifted him with the insight. It gave him the courage he was looking for.

Bryan spent the rest of the afternoon in the woods, talking to his friends, leaning against trees, and watching the forest creatures live life as a community. Each one had a purpose that fit neatly into the tapestry of forest life.

Humans, Bryan decided, get in their own way by over thinking. It was certainly true for him. As the sun dipped lower in the sky, Bryan made his way back home, his rabbit friend leading the way.

Eddie met him partway, appearing on the path in front of him, startling both Bryan and the rabbit. The realization that the animals probably saw the in-between people passed through Bryan's mind before Eddie spoke, and then what Eddie said chased the thought away.

Eddie only stayed a few seconds, but it was enough. He told him that the next day they would do a practice run with Connie, so Bryan might want to get some rest.

As Eddie dissolved away, Bryan thought he heard him giggle. Probably laughing because telling him now meant he probably wouldn't get any sleep at all.

That turned out to be the case. As hard as Bryan tried, he couldn't stop his mind from racing. He kept thinking about his mother and Edith. How well had they known each other? And why was Connie so important that they both had asked him and Eddie to help her? Then he remembered the picture albums.

Even though it was the middle of the night, Bryan slipped on sweatpants and a sweatshirt, some old slippers, and headed to the attic. He hadn't been up there since his mother died.

In the hallway, he jumped up and grabbed the cord hanging from the ceiling, pulled it, and lowered the stairs to the attic to the floor.

Bryan had the headlamp on that he used for walking in the woods in the dark, and it lit his way as he made his way up the ladder. It was a dark, dusty, creepy space.

The boxes he was looking for were stacked together near the attic opening. Grabbing one box at a time, Bryan made his way back down the ladder until he had them all lined up in the hall.

After washing up and grabbing paper towels and a bottle of

spray cleaner, he headed back to the boxes. Inside the boxes were the picture albums that his mother had labeled and put in order.

Only one had pictures lying loose near the top of the box. They were probably photos from after his dad died when his mother had little desire to do things like putting pictures in albums. But at the moment, those weren't the ones he was looking for, so he put that box aside to look through later.

Grateful for his organized mother, Bryan opened the box labeled number one. Inside, the albums were lined up by date. The earliest one was dated 1950. Bryan didn't think his mother knew Edith then, or that it had anything to do with Edith, but he looked through it anyway. Seeing pictures of his mother as a young girl made him smile and tear up. She looked so happy. Was his mother always this happy?

Bryan made his way through the dates until he reached 1960. It was in that album that he hit pay dirt. His mother would have been a freshman in high school that year. Halfway through, Bryan found a picture of her beside another girl. Leaning into each other, laughing at whoever was taking the picture. Underneath the picture, he read, 'Edith Warren and me, May 1960.'

Two beautiful girls, with their lives in front of them. What had happened?

By then, the sun was up, and Bryan made coffee and then went to take a shower and get dressed for the day. If they were doing a practice run today, perhaps he would find answers to some of his questions.

TWENTY EIGHT

While Bryan walked in the woods, Rachel was in Grace's living room, wondering what she had gotten herself into.

Grace had told her to come by at 5:00 p.m. for dinner. She was told not to bring anything. She was their guest. Rachel could meet people, and then afterward, they would talk about what she needed.

Although Rachel arrived at precisely five, everyone else had already arrived and were milling around waiting to say hello.

At first, she felt like running from all the attention, and then she realized it was what she had come for—to be seen, heard, and supported.

And Grace made it comfortable. She introduced Rachel to each person, telling Rachel a little about each one. Grace did it with such ease at first, Rachel didn't notice what Grace was doing. When she did, she leaned in and whispered, "Thank you."

Grace smiled back, knowing what Rachel meant.

The first person Grace introduced Rachel to was Valerie Price. Of course, they had met that morning, but when Grace introduced them this time, she added that Valerie used to be the principal of the school, after moving to Doveland with her husband, who had recently passed away. When a dark cloud passed over Valerie's face at the mention of her husband, Rachel said nothing other than it was a pleasure to see her again.

Standing beside Valerie was her older son, Johnnie. Grace explained that Johnnie was finishing up his schooling at Penn State. When he was home, he helped his mother run the small interior design business that she ran out of her home. Rachel smiled at Johnnie, thinking Johnny was the age of a child she might have had if things had been different.

Moving on, Grace took Rachel to meet Pete Mann and his wife, Barbara. They were in the kitchen, making sure everything was perfect. Rachel had seen both of them at the Diner but had never met them officially. Grace added that Pete and Barbara had bought the Diner a few years before. They had discovered Doveland after Pete picked up a hitchhiker heading to Los Angeles.

"Hitchhiker?" Rachel said, not understanding how a hitchhiker would have brought them to Doveland if the hitchhiker was heading to Los Angeles.

"Grace, that is so confusing," a woman said, coming over to stand next to Pete. She was tall and slim, with sun-streaked brown hair that fell halfway down her back. She was holding the hand of a very handsome man.

The woman stuck out her hand and said, "Hi, I'm, Ava Anders, the hitchhiker, and this is my husband, Evan.

"It's a lengthy story, but the essence of it was I was trying to find my daughter, and afraid to tell anyone that I had one. It all worked out for the best, and I learned the valuable lesson of not trying to do life on my own. Which, I believe, is why you are here."

When Rachel nodded, Ava added, "We're delighted that we are the people you came to for help. Knowing these people," Ava said, waving her hand through the crowd, "you have nothing to worry about."

"Exactly," Pete said, "But first, we eat!"

As they walked to the table, Ava leaned over to Rachel and whispered in her ear. "I know we are a little much. But over time, you'll hear all our stories. However, right now, we are here for you."

Rachel nodded, found her seat at the table, and decided that although she worried about what was coming, it might be the best thing that ever happened to her.

The dinner was delicious. Grace had made her famous spaghetti, and Pete had made garlic toast. As Rachel listened to them all chatting and filling each other in with what was going on with them since the last time they met, she thought perhaps they were doing it for her.

When Ava looked over at her and winked, it startled her. *Had Ava read her mind? Who were these people? Did they all read thoughts? What else did they do? Did they see people like Connie and Eddie too, the same way that Bryan did?*

This time it was Johnny who looked over at her, smiled, and then looked past her shoulder into the living room. Rachel turned but didn't see anyone there.

When she turned back to Johnnie with a questioning look, he said, "A woman is standing there. Do you know her?"

No one seemed surprised at what Johnnie had said, so Rachel asked him to describe who he saw. After Johnny described her as an older woman, graying hair, blue eyes, average height, Rachel answered, "It's probably Connie."

"Well, she's gone now. Most likely surprised I saw her. It takes some in-betweeners time to adjust."

Rachel nodded as if she understood, but she didn't. She had so many questions she didn't know where to start.

Johnny had gone back to eating, so she turned her attention to the rest of the conversation, trying to take it all in but finding herself drifting away, wondering how she ended up talking about what people called ghosts as if they were real.

Well, they are real, Rachel thought. She had seen them.

And if she was crazy, so were all the people at the table. At least she was in friendly company.

Rachel decided to stop worrying and enjoy the meal and the conversations. The time for worrying could come later.

TWENTY NINE

"All right, let's get started," Eddie said to the three of them gathered in Bryan's living room.

Connie, looking more substantial than the last time they saw her, sat in his mother's favorite chair. Bryan couldn't decide if he liked that she was sitting there or not. Or maybe liked wasn't the right word. Was he bothered by her sitting there? Would his mother mind?

Eddie interrupted Bryan's thoughts when he said, "No, she wouldn't. Pay attention."

Rachel had her hand on Bryan's arm so she could see both Eddie and Connie. When she looked as if she would ask what they were talking about, Eddie shook his head. He was in no mood for anyone's questions.

Eddie sighed.

Sometimes he couldn't believe that he had agreed to do this. People were so hard to deal with, so many questions, so much confusion. However, despite his frustration, he understood what Connie was going through and why Rachel wanted to know more about what he did.

Eddie remembered when he first arrived in the in-between. He

was as confused as Connie. Even more so because of how he
died. And although his life with his father was difficult and often
frightening, his mother and grandparents, Lorraine and Ralph,
made up for it.

Besides, right before his mother died, life had just started
getting exciting. He had joined Little League, was learning how to
Rollerblade, and was preparing to go to summer camp. And then
she died. And not long after that, he died too. And when he woke
up, he didn't understand what had happened.

Having been dead for so many years and helping more people
than Eddie could count to pass safely through the in-between, he
knew everyone died and woke up differently.

Usually, older people were more prepared. Unless it was a violent
death, then it was harder. Violent deaths were always harder no
matter what age the people were.

He rarely worked with people who died that way. Someone
wiser than him would be their guide. Even after all these years,
he still had trouble helping some people. It was probably because
he so easily lost his patience. Something else he had promised his
mother to work on. Learn how to be more patient.

There were many reasons some people stayed in the in-between.
Some did because they had unfinished business to attend to, like
Connie. Others didn't realize, or couldn't accept, that they had
died.

Some people made the choice to stay in the different levels of the
in-between. Often they stayed because they found a level where
others who thought like them lived. Or they found people they
had known when they were alive. They would stay with them and
make a fresh life for themselves until they were ready to move on.

Others stayed in the in-between because they couldn't let go of
a tie they had with those still living in the 3D material level of
existence.

Sometimes it was because they wanted to wait for, or watch over, a loved one.

Sometimes it was because a loved one wouldn't let go, which kept the person who died stuck in the in-between.

That was something Eddie had a hard time accepting. He couldn't understand the living who wouldn't let the ones who died move on which harmed the people they claimed to love in the process.

Then there were those like him who stayed to help people having trouble with the transition. Some of them specialized in the help that they gave, like the guides who assisted the animals, or people, who died violently.

These in-betweeners were present at a person or animal's death. He knew a family who lived in the in-between, who specialized in taking care of animals, who died after being hit by a car. They would walk the streets and highways, be there when the animal died, and then take it into their home to heal it before sending it on.

But as with the living, to get help people had to be willing to be helped. Animals usually were, people more often were not. It was the people who carried baggage through their life into their deaths that were the hardest to help.

As they had in life, they fought what was happening, afraid to face truths, unwilling to change. Eddie tried not to work with those people. He had made an exception with Connie because of his mother and Jillyan.

Although Eddie had been present at Connie's passing, she was unable to see him for weeks. Bitter, bored, angry emotions acted like barriers. Until they dissolved or broke down, life after death was difficult the same way it had been in their life before. And Connie had been full of all of those emotions.

But some people moved right through to the light, like his grandparents. Eddie had stayed because his mother, who had been waiting for him, said he would learn how to help others. It was what he would have done if he had lived. With Connie, Eddie was fulfilling his last agreement to help. Then he would join his mother and hopefully his grandparents.

Eddie knew that Connie, Rachel, and Bryan were learning that no one dies; they just move on. Life always lives.

How to live that life was very much a choice, there or here. And that was what his job had been. To give the dead a chance to change what they had chosen in life. And in this case, also help Rachel and Bryan to stop drifting through life.

As if it is okay to squander it, Eddie muttered to himself. *There shouldn't have to be a death to remind people of that, but sometimes that's what it takes.*

The three people in front of him would learn things they might wish they didn't know. But it would be worth it.

Eddie had decided to tell them very little. If he told them too much about where they were going or what they were about to do, they wouldn't pay attention to what was happening. If this was going to work, all three of them had to be present in every moment, without preconceived ideas of what they would do.

He knew that Connie had an idea about what she would have to do.

But then, she could be wrong.

And Eddie wanted that uneasiness to work in her favor, not against her. The sooner she did the right thing, the sooner all of them would be free.

THIRTY

Eddie knew Connie was trying to appear calm. But her twitching foot said otherwise.

He heard the echo of his mother's voice say, "Be patient, Eddie." So he changed his mind about snapping at her for being nervous.

Eddie also realized he was moving too fast.

If he sent Connie back in time now, she would fail. She didn't yet know enough to step back into who she had been over forty years in the past, and still keep the memory of her future death.

She would have to confront what she had done wrong and make an alternative choice. Even with Bryan helping her, it would be too confusing. For anyone, not just Connie.

And if Connie failed, he failed. He never pushed people this hard or this fast before. It was his impatient nature to get this over with.

But it was more than that. Connie's mistake affected him and his mother. It had defined all of their lives and even their deaths. He questioned if he was the right person to help Connie. But he knew his mother wouldn't have asked him to if he wasn't.

Speaking out loud, Eddie said, "Slight change of plan. Instead of physically going into the past, you will only visit it but not be in it.

"You will be an observer, only. If that goes well, we'll move to the next stage. While you are observing, there is nothing that you can do, so don't bother trying. That will come later. Observe carefully. What did you miss before? Don't judge what is happening.

"Bryan, this is Connie's past life. She may get pulled in. Don't let her. Your job is to be the anchor for her."

Turning to Rachel, he said, "And your job is to be the anchor for Bryan. He will still be here with you, just absent from his body. Stay in the now. Can you do that?"

Rachel gulped, turned pale, and nodded yes, hoping that was true.

"Bryan, be sure to check back with Rachel as you make this visit. Practice it. Don't worry about how you do that. It will be obvious. Just don't let your connection to either Rachel or Connie be severed.

"Stay present at all times with yourself. Since you are going back in time, you won't see your body, but you are still connected to it, as long as you don't get sucked into anything. Rachel is your lifeline. Remember that."

As Bryan and Rachel stared at Eddie as if he was crazy, he turned his attention to Connie.

"This may be harder for you. You will see things you didn't see before. I know I keep telling you this, but I want you to really hear me.

"Let me say it again. Don't react. Don't judge. Don't get sucked in.

"Pay attention to Bryan. He will keep you connected to the world as you know it. If you don't enjoy being in the in-between now, you will like it even less if you don't do what I tell you to do.

"And, you may see things that scare you. When you are out of your body, you will see others out of their body too. Like the world you know now, there are evil things out there. Remember. Don't react, don't judge, don't get sucked in."

Rachel thought it was both strange and annoying to be told what to do by a boy of ten, who was technically a 50-year-old ghost, but when Eddie said, "Are you ready?" She forgot everything else but the idea that she was to be present.

Eddie didn't give them a chance to say yes or no, or even to acknowledge what he said.

For Rachel, nothing changed except she could no longer see Connie and Eddie, and Bryan's arm felt different.

For Connie and Bryan, everything changed.

One minute Connie and Bryan were in Bryan's living room, and the next, they were at Edith's house.

The first thing that Connie saw was the calendar on the wall. She remembered seeing the picture of the daffodils on it when they had come back for spring break. It was the spring of 1968.

At first, Connie thought she would be sick—if that were possible as a ghost. She was so disoriented she wanted to reach out and grab something, but couldn't.

She could see herself sitting in Lorraine and Ralph's kitchen, telling them about her plans for the fall.

Connie was aware that Bryan was with her somehow, but as she watched herself, she forgot him. It was all so unreal, seeing herself as she used to be.

She had been so alive and excited.

Edith was getting married. She was looking for a job in the city. She wanted to learn the ropes, and then she would start her own company. Be her own boss. Like Ralph, but bigger, more money, more prestige. More power.

Everyone was so happy. Or were they?

With the distance of time, and knowing what would happen, Connie looked again. Her young self, so arrogant in her happiness. She assumed that everyone was happy for her.

She thought she was pleased for Edith because Edith had snagged the man that she wanted, and she would get the job of her dreams. Both of them would have the life they had talked about, giggled about at night, and planned for as they made their way through school.

But now Connie could see that Ralph was hiding something. Worry? Disappointment? Yes, Loraine said all the right words about being happy for Edith and Connie, but those words didn't reach her eyes.

What had she missed back then? Why hadn't she paid attention? Connie felt a tug and knew that Bryan wanted her to remember why she was there. To observe. Not judge what she was seeing.

Connie watched as Bill came into the kitchen, said good morning, smiled, and said how happy he was for Connie and Edith. But as he reached across the table to hold her hand, this time, Connie felt his sorrow.

Was he sad for her, or Edith, or for both of them? Knowing what she knew now, it could have also been fear.

Bryan tugged again. It was time to see more. She drifted up to Edith's room, where she found Edith still asleep. That was Edith. She liked her sleep. But she was getting married. Shouldn't she be more excited?

Connie had always worried about Edith's decision to marry a rich man so she could have a safe life. Nothing about it appealed to Connie, and they had more than one discussion about it.

But Edith never wavered, and now that she had what she wanted, she was still sleeping?

Something felt wrong. What was it? Out of the corner of her eye, Connie saw movement. A dark shape vanished the minute she glanced its way. Bryan tugged, and she fell backward in space and found herself once again back in Bryan's living room.

Rachel was holding Bryan's hand. He was trembling.

"What was that?" They asked in unison.

THIRTY ONE

"What did you see?" Eddie asked.

Both Connie and Bryan shook their heads, and Bryan said, "I don't know what it was, it just felt wrong. It was like a shadow that moved on its own."

He looked over at Connie, and she nodded in agreement, and then asked, "Was it a person? A thing? Why was it there?"

"I don't know. Those dark things are often there, and most of the time they are not there for you. But you need to know they exist. It could be a person, or a person's thoughts. Or someone who has died and got stuck in the in-between.

"There are black energies like that in the 3D physical world too. But most people don't feel or see them. And people who do, and don't know how to handle their existence, are often treated as if they are insane. It's assumed that whatever they see and hear isn't real. I believe some people in Doveland call it the "There." Since you were both outside of time and the material illusion, you saw what exists in that place more easily."

Rachel asked the next question. "Do you know what or who it was, Eddie? And was it there by coincidence, or because it was hanging around Edith?"

Connie gasped, and both hands flew to her mouth, and she started trembling. Eddie gave her a moment before saying, "Well, I think Connie has an idea what it was. And it has to do with what she has to do when she returns."

Connie didn't answer, just hung her head and began to fade away.

"If you go," Eddie said to her, "nothing changes. You will remain stuck. Your daughter will never know who she is. Edith's wish will go unfulfilled.

"Are you going to be a coward and let everyone down again?"

After a long moment, Connie looked up at Eddie. "So, you know what happened?"

"Part of it. I know my death resulted from what you didn't do. And you knew that, didn't you? It's why you didn't come to the funeral. You felt responsible, and you had already quit living.

"The question now is, are you ready to live again? Do you have the courage to go back and try again? Not everyone gets this chance. It's only because my mom and Bryan's mom requested it that you have it. Are you going to take it or not?"

Connie didn't answer for a long moment. Finally, she just nodded, yes.

"It's not your choice where I am sending you. For this to work, you have to experience it, not remember it," Eddie said.

"But here's a warning. If you stop what happened to you before it happens or while it is going on, you won't have Karla. It's your choice. But just in case you chicken out and don't go through it again, perhaps you want to see Karla before you and Bryan leave for the past."

Connie started to cry again. This time actual tears flowed done her cheek, and Rachel felt her eyes well up too. This was like living in a dream. She was helping people who had died. Why her? And although she didn't know for sure what had happened to Connie, she thought she knew. And to go through that again, knowing what it would be like, that was a nightmare, a living nightmare.

She didn't think she could do it. But then she hadn't had a child. And Connie had. Rachel knew that Connie would do it for Karla.

• • • ● • ● • ● • • •

Karla Matthews stood in her mother's garden and let herself cry. No one could see her. Her mother had designed a beautiful fence that enclosed the entire backyard. The birds loved it because the garden overflowed with bushes, trees, and flowers that fed and sheltered them.

It was also safe from wandering cats. Cats who lived outside and preyed on birds made her mother furious. It was one of the few times Karla would see emotion from her mother. Although cats caused millions of deaths of birds, a fact which made Karla angry too, she knew her mother's anger about predatory cats was more than about them. But Karla didn't know what and never tried to find out. Maybe that made her a terrible daughter.

Her mother had been both a recluse and depressed, which sometimes erupted in anger as long as Karla could remember. She thought that perhaps when she was younger, she had tried to get through to her mother, and then gave up.

But they had a few things in common. They both loved the garden, and they both loved to design things. They had even created some things together, but eventually, one would say the wrong thing, and their brief mother-daughter time would end.

When Connie died, Karla thought she would feel relieved. She wouldn't have to be one of those daughters that had to take care of an old mother. Since she didn't have any siblings or any family she knew about, it would have been her who did all the work. Karla knew people who did that—trying to take care of their own family and their parents at the same time. It was draining, both emotionally and financially.

Karla thought herself lucky that now she had neither. Although she had a few romantic interludes, they never lasted. Probably because, like her mother, she alternated between depression and anger. And in her own way, she was a recluse. She blamed her mother, or she told herself that she did to make it easier on herself.

But the few times that she told herself the truth, she knew that she could have chosen differently. She could have lived a life. It was always there for her, waiting for her to walk into it. But every time it was offered, she pushed it away. And now look at her. Fifty years old. Never married. And no family.

Karla turned away from the garden and made her way into the home where she had lived all her life. Someone wanted to buy it, a young family who could bring this house to life. All she had to do was say yes to the offer and walk away. But she kept stalling. She was here in the house to try to figure out why she wasn't letting it go. Her mother had been gone for over a month. It was time.

Walking upstairs to take one last look at her childhood bedroom, she glimpsed herself in the closet mirror. She had watched herself grow up in that mirror, never understanding what she saw because although she had blue eyes like her mother, she looked nothing like her. Who did she look like? Someone tall with black hair.

The secret about her father had kept them apart. When Karla would ask who he was, Connie would get angry and would stop talking for days. Until finally, they would reach an uneasy truce again.

It was a sad life, Karla thought. For both of them. Could it have been different? Could they have found a way to connect? Maybe they could have connected more with their love of gardening and design. But it was too late. Now she had to decide what to do with herself. Continue with the design shop she had opened? Or let it go, calling it a failure like everything else she had done so far in her life?

Like mother, like daughter, Karla thought. *Failures at life.*

THIRTY TWO

What Karla didn't see, couldn't see, was her mother and a young boy watching her as she cried in the garden and then wandered around the house in a daze. Perhaps it was an unconscious awareness of her mother's presence that had her wondering if she wanted to sell the house. If she didn't sell it, what would she do with it? Live in it? Could she? Would she be able to live there with all the dreadful memories she had of growing up?

"They weren't all bad," Connie whispered. It was painful to finally have the desire to communicate with her daughter and yet have no way to do so. At least not the way she was now in the in-between.

"I'm ready," Connie said, turning to Eddie.

He didn't hear her at first. He was absorbed in watching Karla. If Connie would have just done that one thing, perhaps he and Karla would have known each other.

"Eddie," Connie said louder. "I'm ready."

Back in Bryan's living room, Eddie was all business. He reminded Connie that she would take the place of her past self. That Bryan would be there with her, and that Rachel would keep them both anchored to this time and place.

"Wait," Bryan said. "Still not clear about this. Will I be in the past too? Or a 'ghost' type thing that only Connie can see?"

"And where does the past me go?" Connie interjected.

Eddie shook his head. He was losing his grip. This was the kind of thing he usually spent more time explaining. It was his impatience to get this thing with Connie over with that was causing the problem.

And seeing Karla had done a number on his head. Although he knew that Connie was going back to make things right, he didn't know what would happen when she did.

Since this was the first case he had worked on that directly affected him, he had a tiny niggle of worry that somehow this would change what happened to him. What if he wasn't born? Or maybe he wouldn't die young. Then what would happen?

Get over yourself, Eddie said to himself. *The answers for you are the same for everyone.*

"Eddie?" Rachel said. "Are you all right?"

"Sure. I was just thinking I didn't explain this well to all of you. Here's the simplest way to tell you, although you must know that it's more complicated than this. But our minds can't quite grasp it all, so you'll just have to go with it for now."

Everyone nodded in agreement.

"You know that there are alternative realities."

"Wait," Bryan said. "How can you assume that we know this? Who has ever proved it?"

"Look at what is happening right now, Bryan. Are you talking to two dead people? That is an alternative reality to what most people experience.

"Yes, there are many ways to see this. Life never dies, so the people we think are dead, aren't. They go somewhere. Where?

"People made up the alternative realities of heaven and hell. Then there is what we are calling the in-between. Or what your friends in Doveland call the There.

"The thing is, everything that will happen has happened—somewhere. There are unlimited alternative realities, alternative dimensions. Call it what works for your brain to grasp the idea that there is no linear time, and that there are infinite possibilities. But we are dealing with just this one. We have enough trouble dealing with this one without worrying about more than that.

"Although, I know that the people in Doveland that Rachel met with have dealt with at least two of them. But that's neither here nor There. Ha. Made a joke."

When no one laughed, Eddie returned to his stoic self, which Rachel found confusing. He looked ten. He acted ancient. When Eddie winked at her, Rachel smiled back. Maybe not so stoic or ancient after all.

"Okay, here's the simple answer to your questions. Connie, when you go back to the past, you will return as yourself, and with the memories of who you are now.

"Your past self will be off in another dimension or reality, where your past self didn't exist before. Yes, it changes that one. Yes, it makes another branch of reality, but we can't be worried about that. Especially since technically everything we do creates another one. Infinite, remember?

"As for you, Bryan. You did not exist then, well, at least not in that form."

When Rachel started to ask about that, Eddie stopped her.

"No, not important right now. If we keep talking about this, Connie will never get into the past.

"Bryan will be a spirit, or ghost—whatever you want to call it—just as he was when you did your angel impersonation, Connie.

"You can talk to each other if you wish, but mostly just think of him as your guide. You will see him sometimes. Other times you may not. Doesn't matter. He will still be able to hear you.

"If things go wrong, Bryan will pull—so to speak—on his lifeline back to Rachel. Since his body will remain here with her, he'll be living a normal life. That is if talking to someone in the past, and showing up for them, is normal."

"Why can't you go with me, Eddie? Why do we need all these different people involved? Not that I am not grateful," Connie quickly added, "Just why do we need them?"

Eddie sighed again. "Well, for one thing, you are not the only person I am helping in the in-between. And for another, there are those who believe that I wouldn't be objective. After all, this is my life too that you are messing around with.

"Do it right, and we all experience what should have happened if you would have done the right thing the first time. Do it wrong, and you and I, and who knows who else, could be worse off than we are now."

Rachel shook her head at Eddie. "That doesn't help, Eddie. Connie needs encouragement, not your sarcasm or anger."

Eddie knew Rachel was right. No wonder people wondered if he could do this.

"Sorry, Connie," Eddie said, still with a twinge of anger in his voice. But Connie was too nervous and scared to notice. Eddie's heart softened a little. One mistake, who could blame her for one mistake. Everyone makes them, including him.

This time when he said, "I'm sorry," he meant it. Connie looked over at him and smiled.

"Are you ready?" Eddie asked.

When all three people nodded yes, Connie and Eddie vanished.

Bryan jerked back in his seat, paused, looked around the room, and said, "Oh, man. I feel very weird. I don't know if I like this at all."

For a moment, Eddie returned, without Connie, and said, "Get used to it. This is now your life."

Turning to Rachel, Eddie smiled and gave her a little bow, and then he was gone again, leaving behind him more questions than he had answered.

THIRTY THREE

Connie screamed. Luckily, there was no one to hear her. She was alone. She looked down at her hands and screamed again. Then started laughing. She wasn't looking at age-spotted and slightly swollen knuckles on each hand. They were young again. They didn't hurt.

She squeezed her eyes shut and then opened them again. Yes, they still looked young. She pushed herself up from the tiny table they used as a desk and looked around. She was in their apartment across the street from the college. Connie fell back into her chair, savoring the fact that she could feel her chair.

She stood again, marveling at how easy it was to stand up and sit down. She hadn't noticed how hard it had become for her to move.

While part of Connie's brain was processing her newly gained feeling of youth, the other part was trying to place herself in time.

When she had visited Loraine and Ralph at their house, it had been early spring. Now she could see all the trees on the campus were fully leafed out. She loved that view, and for a moment, she wondered why she had never come back to visit.

But then Connie remembered why, and all the pain and

resulting sorrow came flooding back, and she stumbled back into the chair.

She remembered that she was dead now somewhere, in some timeline or dimension or alternate reality of life. She couldn't think straight.

Where was Edith? What if she came in now, how would she talk to her? Would Edith know the difference?

She couldn't just say, "Hey, Edith. I'm dead now. It's over fifty years in the future. Terrible things happened. I can't tell you about them. I'm here to fix them if I can."

No, there was no one to talk to about it. No help at all. And then Connie remembered. There was Bryan. She was supposed to be able to speak to him. How? Did Eddie forget to tell her? Maybe all she had to do was say his name. Did it have to be out loud?

Although she was alone, Connie whispered, "Bryan?"

Connie could feel something loud coming towards her. Like an airplane flying directly at her, except it was in her brain. It hit the center of her skull and she felt a flash of blinding light.

"Ouch!" Connie heard Bryan say.

"Ouch? What do you mean, ouch? I'm the one who got hurt. What are you doing? Is that what it will be like? I thought you were supposed to help me, not give me a case of fright and a headache."

Bryan's faint outline appeared against the wall that she and Edith had painted black, thinking it would make their apartment stylish.

She and Edith had argued over it, and as always, she had won. Even now, knowing what she knew, she still liked that black wall. Even Edith admired it after she got used to it.

And now it showed up the slightly white outline of Bryan's body. The inside of him was translucent, which made the wall turn gray. Also a lovely color, Connie randomly thought to herself.

"No. Oh. Sorry. I bumped my knee on the kitchen cabinet when you called. I didn't know it would be like that. Okay. This is just plain freaky. I can see you, and you are solid—like a real person. I don't mean you weren't a person before, but you were quite see-through."

"You mean, how you are now?" Connie said, pointing to him. Bryan looked down.

"Oh, God. That's too creepy. What do you want? I want to go home. This will take some adjustment. I can't feel my knee now. I wonder if that's a good thing." Bryan's form spun around, so he was looking into the wall. Then he turned back.

"Oh good. I can see Rachel. It's good. We're good. What is it you wanted?"

Bryan sat down, and Connie assumed he had sat on one of the kitchen chairs, but she couldn't see it. Funny, that only Bryan came through.

"I supposed I don't want anything, except to see if I could really reach you." The phone on her desk rang, and Connie looked at it as if it was something from another planet.

Oh. A phone. Yes, pick it up and say hello, she said to herself as she reached out for the phone.

Bryan remained seated, silhouetted against the black wall, and Connie nodded at her phone and said, "Okay," and then looked at the phone in her hand again as if trying to remember how to hang it up.

"Put that thing you are holding back on the phone cradle," Bryan said, wondering how come he knew what an old phone looked like, and she didn't. Probably because she was so disoriented.

"Who was it?"

"Edith. She says she and Theo are going out to dinner after they finish studying. I'm supposed to go out with them."

"Okay. So you don't need me anymore," Bryan said and disappeared.

Connie wanted to yell back that she did still need him, but he was already gone. How was she going to act when she saw Edith and Theo?

She remembered that dinner. They laughed and joked and talked about the wedding. Theo was his charming self, and he even had Connie taking a sip of wine.

What did she wear then? Did it matter if she wore the same thing? Was this happening again, or for the first time? Or was it both at the same time? So did it matter that she wore the same thing, or said the same thing this time around?

Connie decided that was all too confusing and the only thing she had to do was not let on that she knew what was coming. She had to pretend that she liked Theo enough to be around him instead of being terrified.

Wait. She wouldn't have been terrified yet. Connie remembered what Eddie had said. She had to go through with what happened. Could she do it?

In her head, she heard Bryan say, "You can. Oh, that was cool. I see that I don't always have to come there for you to hear me. We can talk this way. Gotta go, Eddie just showed up."

A second later, Connie heard Bryan again

"Oh, one more thing. This is good. If I don't come there, I can't see you. So if you don't see me, I don't see you. Thought you might want to know that. You know for privacy and everything."

Connie felt a slight easing of pressure in her head and realized that had been Bryan. She'd get used to it. She grabbed a pair of jeans off the bed and slipped on a clean blouse. That would do for dinner.

A glance in the mirror reminded her that she had that dirty blond hair again. No longer gray. No more wrinkles and saggy skin.

An old woman's thoughts in a youthful woman's body. This should be interesting.

THIRTY FOUR

Since where they would have dinner was just a few blocks away, Connie decided that she would take a walk around town first. She passed the little tobacco shop where she used to buy licorice, smiled at the memory, walked on, and then turned back and went inside.

She was young again. She could enjoy it.

The shop was just as she remembered it. The sweet smell of tobacco hung over everything. Jars of licorice lined up on the counter. She asked for five black and five red pieces. The older man she could barely see behind the counter took them out of the jars and handed them to her in a white paper bag.

"Enjoy them, Connie," the man said, and Connie smiled, wishing she could remember his name. It had been over fifty years for her. For him, it was probably only a day or two since she had last stopped in.

Connie glimpsed herself in the door's reflection as she left, and for a moment, forgot it was her. She stared at the young, slim woman, said "excuse me," and then realizing she was looking at herself, laughed, and then turned back to wink at the man behind the counter so he would think it was a joke. It worked. He smiled and lifted his hand.

Strange that she thought he was old when she was much older than him. Connie wondered if he was still alive. Probably not.

The rest of the walk through town was the same. Memories would flood back, and Connie had to keep placing them in a separate room in her mind. She had to see the world as if she was twenty-two, ready to start a new, beautiful, and exciting life.

Heading to the Tavern she kept saying to herself, you can do this!

Looking back at the campus, she saw Edith and Theo getting ready to cross the street. Like most students, they crossed wherever they wanted to, dodging cars, and smiling at the ones that honked at them.

Connie looked at them, remembering what a handsome couple they had made. Theo, tall, slim with dark hair combed away from his face, was looking very preppy.

Even then, Connie thought he was too styled, too perfectly put together. Back then, she had thought he looked in the mirror each morning and imagined himself as the handsome, charming man ready to take over the world,

Now she knew that was exactly what he did every morning. And noon. And night.

Stop it, she said to herself.

She turned her attention to Edith, holding on to Theo's arm, alternately smiling at the drivers and Theo. So happy. So innocent. Edith caught the eye of all the men, young and old, with her shining ebony hair and curvy body.

Theo beamed. Why wouldn't he? He had captured the woman of every man's dreams.

Connie sighed and looked down at herself. She wasn't that and never had been. Too skinny, mousy blondish hair, too short, and too opinionated to be any man's dream girl.

She thought she hadn't cared. But what if she did? What if her biased look at Theo had caused the problem? What if she had been jealous, and that's why he did what he did?

When the two of them reached Connie, Theo bent down to kiss her on her cheek, Connie recoiled slightly. Both Theo and Edith looked at her with puzzled looks on their faces.

To cover up her reaction, she hooked her arm into Theo's other arm and said, "I'm starving. Let's eat."

Later that night, as she lay in her bed looking at the ceiling, Connie realized that everything that happened that night was just as she remembered it.

But that fact worried her. Connie knew that all memories are false. That every time someone recalls a memory, they unconsciously alter it. When she first heard that idea, she dismissed it. Couldn't be true. Then what was the point of having a memory? She didn't have the answer to that question, but she came to believe the studies that showed how false memories are.

So that night, did she relive a false memory, or what really happened?

What if when she got to the part where she made the wrong choice, she made the wrong choice again? Given all that could go wrong, how would she ever get it right?

· · · · ● · ● · ● · · ·

Eddie had lied. Well, not lied completely. He did have some other jobs to do in the in-between. But they were easy. At least compared to the one with Connie. All he had to do was greet the newly dead person and help them to their next stage of life.

Not everyone needed an escort to their destination. That was a good thing, because there were not enough people in the in-between to do that. Thankfully, most people had friends and family waiting for them who would help with the acclimation.

But some people couldn't accept that they had died, so they didn't see the people waiting for them. They wandered around confused and often angry. Which made it worse.

Those were the cases he didn't like to take, although if it was busy, and no one else could, he did.

Then there were those like Connie, who had to stay in the in-between until they completed some unfinished business.

Right now, other than Connie, the only cases he had were the confused ones. They were often easily guided to where they could get more help. Sometimes, they went directly to the light once they accepted what had happened.

Eddie always liked those moments. It made his life in the in-between worth it. He treasured those moments when the lost were reunited with their loved ones and remembered who they were.

He always heard beautiful music when that happened, but he thought that his imagination supplied that effect. He knew that as in life, in death, people saw what they thought they were supposed to see—or had accepted as truth.

So Eddie had lied about why he would not help Connie directly. But he didn't consider it lying. He just wasn't filling Connie or Bryan in on all the details yet. It was better that way.

Eddie wanted Bryan to find himself as he helped Connie. It was the other thing he had promised—this time to Jillyan, Bryan's mother.

So far, Eddie was pleased with both Connie and Bryan. They had done well for the first day. Eddie knew it was confusing. If he thought about it too much himself, he got confused, too, understanding the great mystery, some people called God? Well, he wasn't there yet, so he didn't expect others to be there either.

Eddie thought since Connie was doing so well on her own, perhaps Bryan would like to play angel. He had the perfect event in mind for him.

THIRTY FIVE

When Eddie went to see Bryan, he and Rachel were already in bed. Because Eddie told Rachel that she needed to stay close to Bryan, she had gone home and packed a suitcase.

Neither of them complained about her staying at Bryan's house, but the way they were getting together was not as either of them had once imagined.

Rachel was staying in Bryan's parents' bedroom. Following his mother's request, Bryan had cleaned it out after she died, and donated all her clothes to Goodwill. He had kept only a few things—a bottle of perfume, and framed pictures of the family. Everything else was gone, so it was a clean slate for Rachel.

Bryan wondered if his mother knew Rachel would need a room and decided it was highly possible.

Rachel had gone to bed early, claiming exhaustion. Eddie knew she must be tired. All of this was so new to both of them. She had told him a little about her meeting with the Doveland crowd. She said that it had been both supportive and frightening. She was happy that they were there, but wondered what she had gotten herself into.

Bryan had headed to his bedroom not much later, but found he was too keyed up and too tired to sleep. A dichotomy, he realized, like the one with Rachel. He wanted her in his house. But not the way it was happening. He wanted more.

Rachel had always been the one for him, but he could never say that out loud. He had always been afraid that he wasn't good enough for her. Now they were working together, making him more aware of how he felt about her. And yet he was still too much of a useless coward to tell her so.

That was the state Bryan was in when Eddie found him. Lying on his bed, pretending to sleep, but mentally beating himself up for not speaking up. Even now, after all these years. *He was a grown man, for Pete's sake.*

When Bryan saw Eddie standing beside the bed, he shrieked, making him feel more ridiculous than ever. *Who shrieks like that,* Bryan groaned to himself.

"Well," Eddie answered Bryan's unspoken thoughts. "Most everyone shrieks when a spirit startles them. Not that you aren't an idiot, but that's different from being useless. That you are not. Since you can't sleep, do you want to have some fun?"

"Fun? Do you and I have the same idea of what is fun and what is not?"

"Probably not. But even so, how about testing out something to prove to yourself that you are not useless?"

Bryan didn't know what Eddie was suggesting, but he wanted to say no, and yet doing something new excited him. *There's that dichotomy again,* he thought.

"Sure why not," he made himself say.

Before he got the word "not" out, they were gone.

Having watched Connie's excursions to other places, Bryan immediately recognized what was happening, and his exhaustion faded away. He was excited and worried, but his curiosity overrode it all. What would happen? Was he going to help someone?

"I get to be an angel?" Bryan asked, his face lit up.

Eddie stared at him and smiled. If this was what it took to get Bryan into life, he could use him more often. Funny, how helping dead people made Bryan feel alive. But Eddie didn't say any of what he was thinking. Instead, he pointed.

All Bryan could see was what looked like a middle-class neighborhood. Most of the houses were dark, and the only light was a street lamp at every corner. He looked again and saw a man walking down the sidewalk. Well, not so much walking as shuffling. The man was staring at his feet and moving about as slowly as someone could and still be walking.

"Talk to him," Eddie said, and then disappeared.

Bryan was more than disappointed. He thought he would get to save someone from a speeding car the way that Connie had, or rescue someone from a fire. Something exciting.

"So you can be a hero?" Bryan heard Eddie ask him.

Yes, he thought to himself, *so I can be a hero. At least I am honest about that.*

A gaggle of geese flew overhead, making so much noise the young man looked up and stopped in his tracks when he saw Bryan.

"Oh, sorry," he mumbled, "I didn't see you. Sorry."

Bryan looked down at himself and realized that he wasn't just drifting like a ghost; he was solid. At least he looked that way to the man in front of him.

"Oh, hey, my fault," Bryan said, "I was just out for a walk and not paying attention. Mind if I walk with you?"

The man shrugged, and the two of them started down the street together. For blocks, neither one spoke. Finally, the young man asked Bryan why he was out walking.

Bryan decided that he might as well tell this guy about his fear of being nobody, living his life without purpose, never telling the woman he had loved his whole life that he loved her, that he would die a failure because so far he had acted as if he wasn't alive.

He didn't know what came over him. It was as if all the pent-up thoughts and emotions came gushing out. Maybe it was because he was talking to a stranger. Bryan felt embarrassed that he couldn't shut up, but kept talking anyway.

The young man listened, only asking a question or two to keep Bryan talking. Somewhere along the way, they ended up on a bench in a small neighborhood park, and Bryan kept talking, and the man kept listening.

Finally, Bryan ran out of words and turning to the man sitting beside him said, "I don't know why we ran into each other, but dang it, you have helped me. I never told anyone all that stuff. I feel so much better. Lighter somehow. It's like you were put here to help me."

"No," the man said, standing. For the first time, Bryan could see his face, the streetlight shining on it.

"No, you helped me, thank you."

He reached out and shook Bryan's hand, gave him a shy smile, and walked away, no longer shuffling.

Bryan watched him go, wondering who was being the angel that night.

Later, back in bed, he fell asleep still not knowing, but grateful for the chance to help someone else in some small way, and aware that he had received much more than he had given in doing so.

In the dark, Eddie smiled to himself.

THIRTY SIX

When Bryan finally woke up, Rachel had already gone. She had left a note on the kitchen table that she was heading to the coffee shop. He could join her if he wanted to.

He didn't. He had things to think over.

First, he checked in with Connie but found her still sleeping. He wasn't sure what the rules were about being able to see into Connie's life.

He could tell by the mess in the tiny space they called a living room that Edith and Theo were probably in the other bedroom. He was tempted to look. He knew that whatever had happened involved the two of them. Maybe he should know more?

But he stopped himself. That was spying for no reason except personal curiosity, not something he wanted to get in the habit of indulging. Not knowing for sure how this all worked, he also worried that it would change something that shouldn't be changed, and it would be his fault. Not something he imagined was his fault, but actually his fault. It was a terrifying thought. He hoped that Connie could keep it together.

While he dressed, Bryan drank a cup of coffee, ate a piece of toast, and then added a bottle of water and a food bar to a small pack he wore when he was planning to stay in the woods for a while. And he was. If Connie needed him, she would reach out, and Eddie always knew where to find him.

He left a note for Rachel telling her where he had gone. It was the first time since his mother's death when he had to let someone know where he was.

Bryan smiled to himself, surprised to find how happy he was that he was not alone anymore.

· · · ● · ● · ● · · ·

Rachel sat on the park bench listening to the morning chorus of birds, marveling at its beauty. It was early, and she was the only one in the tiny park. It would be bustling in a few hours, but right now, it was just her and the birds.

She was waiting for Valerie. Valerie and her two sons lived in the only house set around the traffic circle that surrounded the park. The rest of the buildings were stores, the bank, a gas station, the Diner, and of course, the coffee shop.

Grace had told her that Valerie's house used to be a bed-and-breakfast, but after her husband died, Valerie quit being the principal of the high school and turned half her home into a design studio.

As far as Rachel knew, it was quite a success. Along with running a local interior design business, Valerie ran a craft website that sold handmade items made by people who lived in the area.

Sitting in the park, Rachel was in the center of Doveland. The four roads that led to the traffic circle around the park were from the four directions. That made it easy to know where you were going, something she had always loved about Doveland. It was hard to get lost.

South of the circle was a hardware store and a bar. The north road led to a new arts school located on a site that used to be a hippie community. While the school was being built, the town discovered the graves of four young women and that led to the discovery that their beloved town doctor, Dr. Joe, was a monster hiding in plain sight. It was Grace and her friends who had uncovered what Dr. Joe had done.

Rachel was sure Grace and her friends were at least partly responsible for how quickly the town had healed from the revelation. One of Ava's friends, Craig Lester, who was part of the group who moved to Doveland, was now the new town doctor, and the new man in Valerie's life.

The arts school transformed into an arts camp in the summer. A woman named Emily and her recent husband, Josh, ran it together. Rachel wished it had been around when she was young. But she had heard they had adult classes. Maybe she should try them out.

The road leading west went by Ava and Evan's home. It also led to the town of Concourse. Hank Blaze—another of Ava's friends—and a crew of high school students with the help of Hank's construction company, had built a bike path alongside the road that traveled the entire way to Concourse. Someday she would have to take it. Maybe she could convince Bryan to go with her.

The road to the east led to a lake. Besides being a popular summer destination, it had been another burying place for some victims of Dr. Joe's experiments.

Yes, the town had secrets. Even though she had lived in Doveland her entire life, she had not been part of those secrets, although she had her own. She knew Dr. Joe, for example. That was not unusual. He had been everyone's doctor. He had helped her through her childhood and was the person she had gone to when she had a decision to make that haunted her still. With all that, how had she not noticed that he was evil?

It worried her, and it scared her. Evil had lived among them, and until Grace and her friends had come to town, no one knew. Or if they did, they had said nothing. Which was worse, that she hadn't noticed, or that people had noticed and didn't speak up?

Rachel knew that saying yes to what Bryan needed had brought her into the center of yet another old mystery centered in Doveland. It was giving her a chance to wake up. She wanted to be the kind of person who spoke up when there was a problem. And she was tired of pretending that she had it all together. After this Connie thing was over, she and Bryan had some talking to do,

Rachel was so lost in thought that she didn't notice Grace until she felt the bench shift under Grace's weight.

Grace handed her a coffee made just as she liked it and said, "Sorry, I didn't mean to startle you, but when I saw you sitting here, I thought I would join you before the shop gets busy. This is my favorite spot to watch the world go by."

Rachel nodded and sipped her coffee. It didn't surprise her that Grace remembered how she liked it. Grace was like the park bench. At the center of everything. A safe place to see and be seen.

Rachel knew that a few years before, a man had passed away one night on the bench. He had come to town to find a long-lost sister. She had died before he found her, but his arrival had brought many mysteries to light. There was an excellent outcome for that story. Josh had found his long-lost love, Emily, while searching for his grandfather, the man on the bench.

Yes, Grace and the bench have known both sorrow and joy, Rachel thought.

Across the street, Valerie's door opened. She waved and headed to the coffee shop. Grace and Rachel followed her.

Rachel knew that she would tell them about her first day being an anchor for Bryan and Connie, and they would provide both a listening ear and guidance if she needed it.

She wasn't sure why she had waited so long to reach out to other people, but happy that she had finally learned the value of a community of friends.

Imagine that. She had found it right here in her hometown.

THIRTY SEVEN

The next week Connie struggled. Not with what she thought would cause her problems. Connie struggled because it was over fifty years in the past.

When she wanted to call someone, there was no effortless way to do it. It took time. She had to find a phone, find their phone number in the phone book, and then hope the person she was calling was home. If she wanted to look something up, she had to go to the library and search for it.

How in the world had they ever lived then, Connie wondered. *Probably because they didn't know about what was coming.*

But she did, and the way things were in the past was making her crazy. She had to hold a book in her hand and turn the pages. And read magazines and newspapers that were entirely out of date. Not because they weren't reporting the news correctly, but with the wisdom of hindsight, they had missed so much of what was really going on.

The novelty of remembering how life used to be wore off quickly. The problem of adjusting to a slower lifestyle, and lack of information, was difficult. What made it worse was she had arrived in her past body and past life just as they were taking finals.

Her test results didn't matter that much. She had good enough grades to graduate. But her study habits had deteriorated, and the answers to the tests were often incorrect given what she knew now. But since she was in 1968, she had to answer it as they thought it was. All of it was driving her crazy.

She might have hidden away in a small town, barely living her adult life, but it was more living than what this new Connie felt was going on in the past. But slowly, she adjusted to it, at least enough so she wasn't constantly looking for her phone to find out where she was, or to find out what she needed to know, or to text Edith. She even remembered to wind her watch.

She learned to check what she was saying, so she didn't say things like, "Google it," or "text me," or even phrases like "Black Lives Matter." Luckily Edith was so wrapped up in Theo she barely registered the differences in Connie, and no one else was close enough to her to notice.

Except Bill. When he came to their graduation.

Everyone came to their graduation. Well, everyone in Edith's family. Connie had never seen or heard from her father again, a fact for which she was grateful. But now Connie could admit that she was angry about it, too. It was irrational, and she didn't like that about herself.

Her friends at the trailer park hadn't come either. She had stopped writing to them, so they didn't know she was graduating, and even if they had known, they wouldn't have come.

Now that she had more wisdom, Connie knew that was her fault. They didn't come because it worried them that they would embarrass her.

I should have known better, she told herself. That was a constant refrain for Connie in her twenty-two-year-old body and seventy-three-year-old mind. She should have known better.

It was a struggle not to change what she had done. She almost went back to see the women, especially Mama Woo. She had packed her car for a visit until she remembered that she couldn't change things.

There was only one thing she had to do differently, and that hadn't happened yet, and might not if she messed around with her past self.

Graduation day had been a perfect summer day. Soft white clouds floated above the ceremony. A light breeze was blowing, so they never got too hot. The first time around, Connie had barely remembered the day. It was just one more step in her life plan.

This time she felt every moment. This time hearing her name called brought her to tears. She savored the hugs from Edith and her family. Theo was with his family for the graduation, for which she was grateful. Even then, she had disliked his parents. Now she had to work hard to hide her disdain for them.

This time, Connie reveled in the feeling of walking to the stage to get her diploma. That diploma had hung on her wall for years until she found she was too embarrassed to look at it. It was a constant reminder of what she could have done with her life.

This time, as she watched all the graduation caps fly into the clear blue sky, she laughed out loud with the joy that came over her. She had done it. With the help of friends, she had done it. How had she forgotten that? How had she become so lost that she thought she could walk away from them?

Connie shook herself and smiled at Lorraine and Ralph. She hugged them so hard they almost fell over. She decided these minor things she was doing couldn't possibly change anything.

Telling them how much they meant to her would not change the future. She hoped.

Because she had to do it. She had to let them know. In the past, she had broken their hearts, and she would do it again because she had to, but that day Connie wanted to tell them how much she loved them.

Bill kept looking at her as if he had never seen her before. Connie knew that, in a way, he hadn't.

This was Connie from the future, living in Connie from the past's body. Bill asked her more than once if something was going on with her, but she just shook her head and said that she was happy to be graduating.

Then she lied some more and said she was happy because Edith was getting married.

"It's just what Edith wants and isn't Theo the perfect catch?"

She had never said that in the past. And Bill knew she didn't mean it.

He shook his head and said, "You're lying to me about more than how you feel about Theo, Connie. Something is different about you. What's going on?"

Connie looked Bill straight into his blue eyes and said, "No, everything is okay. I am just hyped up over graduation and the wedding."

Bill took her hand and stared right back. "You are still lying. You know you can tell me anything."

Connie knew she could. She had back then, too. Now, seeing him again, Connie felt an overflowing love for him. He had secrets she kept for him as he had for her. She knew he had years of pain to work through, but if all went well this time around, he would once again end up with the love of his life.

The urge to tell Bill the entire truth was powerful. Would he understand that she was not the Connie he knew, but a future one? Would he tell her then he hated her for what she had done? For what she had taken away from him?

Connie didn't know. Instead, she rose on her tiptoes and kissed him on the cheek, whispering, "You know I love you, Bill."

They touched foreheads, and for that moment, all was right with the world.

Connie knew it wouldn't last long.

THIRTY EIGHT

The next month flew by. Bryan checked in with Connie every evening as Eddie had told him to. Bryan had asked why it was necessary. Wouldn't Connie call him if she was in trouble or needed him?

Eddie had answered with a clipped voice, "Just do it."

So he had. And after a few weeks of doing so, Bryan could see why it was necessary. Sometimes when he checked in with her, it would startle Connie as if she didn't know who he was.

It seemed to Bryan that Connie was forgetting that she was there for a reason. It worried him that the memory that she was the Connie from the future had sometimes faded into the background.

Or at least that was how it appeared to Bryan. Eddie had gone somewhere and not come back, so the only person Bryan could talk to about it was Rachel. Now Bryan understood why Eddie had insisted that Rachel be part of the plan. Not that he wasn't grateful for the arrangement. He was ecstatic about it. But he hadn't understood that Rachel would not only be the grounding for when he was with Connie, but in everyday life.

Rachel gave him a place to talk over what it felt like to be out of the body and back in time. Not only when he was checking in with Connie, but when he was helping other people. Once Eddie had shown him how to assist people when he left his material body behind, he often found himself in situations where he could do something.

It amazed Bryan that the people he helped—if they saw him—thought he was an angel. Bryan knew he wasn't. He was an ordinary man. It was Rachel who said that was what angels were, ordinary people who did kind things for others. He just happened to be able to intervene in some situations where no one else could. But everyone could be an angel to others in daily life.

Listening to Rachel, Bryan almost had to bite his tongue to stop himself from calling Rachel his angel. But he thought she probably knew. Still, he had promised himself that he would do this thing with Connie before addressing his increasing acceptance that he had always loved Rachel and never wanted to be without her again.

A successful mission with Connie would give him the confidence he needed to ask Rachel to marry him. Until then, he had to be content knowing that Rachel wasn't going anywhere. She had promised Eddie, and one thing Bryan knew about Rachel is that she kept her promises.

Bryan's concern about Connie was justified. Connie was often startled when Bryan checked in with her. Sometimes hours would go by where she forgot that she had come from the future. Connie found that adjusting to the past became more manageable every day. Bryan's intervention every evening sometimes made her mad. And when she was thinking clearly, that reaction worried her. She knew that she was there to correct what she had done, not become part of the past.

Eddie had never told her what would happen if she forgot why she was there. But she assumed it became another variable in the multiple universes of infinite possibilities. Would that matter? Why not just let this life play out the way it was going? Someday she might actually forget that she used to be someone else.

The ease with which she was accepting those ideas sometimes terrified her. Other times she would shrug and say to herself, so what. To get back to her mission, she would think about Karla. Or Edith and what would happen to her if she didn't remember why she was there.

An enormous part of the reason that Connie's memory of the future was fading from her head was the wedding preparation. After graduation, they all threw themselves into getting ready. Even though Theo's mother kept hijacking Edith's plans, they still had plenty to do.

Connie's primary function turned out to be a sounding board for Edith's feelings about Theo, the wedding, Theo's parents, and her future. She was also the errand girl. Whatever Edith needed, Connie would rush to the store to buy it.

That's when she missed how it used to be when she could go to her computer and order things, and they would show up in a few days.

Now, no one had ever heard of a computer. Well, not personal ones. They knew there were refrigerator-sized behemoths that hummed and blinked called computers and people doing calculations for NASA called computers, but it had nothing to do with daily life.

Connie's frustration with how hard things were to get done helped her in one way. It helped keep her grounded in who she was and why she was there. Eddie had warned her about not using her knowledge about what would happen to make life better for her future self, like investing in stocks she knew would rise.

She couldn't do that on her own anyway, since in 1968, women needed a man to open the account and a man to make the trades.

She could ask Bill, but then would have to explain why she wanted to take her tiny savings account and put it into McDonald's stock. He would ask questions she couldn't answer.

And besides, it would break the rules she had agreed to with Eddie.

During the month before the wedding, Connie stayed away from Theo as much as possible. But it wasn't always easy. Edith wanted her to be part of everything.

The tension between Connie and Theo grew whenever they were in the same room. Connie knew Theo for what he was underneath all that simpering charm. She had suspected it then, but now she knew it.

Having to hide her hatred was easier than hiding her fear. She flinched when he came near. She glared at him, and he at her. She wanted to take something heavy and bash him over the head with it.

One night she asked Bryan if he thought she was making an unknown future because of her knowledge of what would happen—what she would let happen because it had to. Neither of them knew the answer, and Eddie was not around to tell them.

So Connie flopped back and forth between forgetting who she was and why she was there, to remembering with such force she was afraid she would do something that would jeopardize all their lives.

Sometimes as Connie lay awake in the Warren's spare bedroom, she thought she could feel that dark shape that she and Bryan had seen when they had visited the house the first time.

But when she looked at it directly, it would vanish, leaving in its wake a feeling of dread and despair.

It occurred to Connie that perhaps it was her memories haunting her. She wasn't sure if that made the apparition more or less terrifying.

THIRTY NINE

Theodore Prince stood in front of the mirror and smiled at himself. He raked his glossy black hair away from his face with his fingers, the gesture an exact copy of what he had seen an actor in a movie do. It was very effective in giving him the look he wanted.

Theo straightened his suit jacket even though it didn't need it. Tailored suits costing thousands of dollars fit without adjustments. But that movement too was something he had seen done by the head of a fortune 500 firm. He adopted the look and the move.

Then he shot his cuffs, so they peaked out just enough to show off the subtle glow of his onyx cuff links. From shining shoes to his blue eyes fitted with blue contacts he didn't need but wore to make his eyes pop, to his smooth unlined skin with the laugh lines in the right places, Theo was perfect, and he knew it. He made sure of it.

His look perfected, Theo moved on to making faces. Not weird faces. Faces that would look like an emotion he wanted people to think he was feeling.

A slight smile of amusement. A wide smile of delight. Then an understanding look. The "something has moved me" expression. Then a look of profound understanding that perhaps included an unshed tear.

The practice didn't take long. Theo could move through the range of emotions within minutes. He had been practicing those emotions every day since he was a young boy, since the day he had overheard his nanny whispering to his mother that there might be something wrong with the boy. He was vacant. He never showed emotion.

His mother, Virginia, didn't care. But Theo did. Even then, he knew that he was different. Not that he cared either. But he was an aware child, so he acted on what he heard.

Now that he was older, Theo knew that he registered as a genius. He was reading by the time he was three. Being smart had made things so much easier. School was useless, but he did it because it was necessary to move on in life. But the smarts that he also had was the awareness that being different could get him in trouble, and that was not something he wanted. Because as long as he could remember, he had desires that he had to hide. And the best way to hide them was in plain sight.

So he couldn't appear to be different. Grateful for what he overheard, Theo did two things.

First, he began studying people's faces, in actual life, on TV, and in movies, and then he copied what he had seen. The result was his father, Joseph, who had mostly ignored him to that point, began to pay attention to him.

Theo knew that it had disappointed his father that his son was so strange. So when he appeared to be getting better, he included Theo in more of his life. As Theo got older, he joined his father at work, which Theo loved. It gave him a chance to study other adults and how they acted and to emulate their actions and emotions. It also gave him a training ground for getting whatever he wanted when he wanted it.

Because the second thing Theo had done after he overheard the nanny that day was get her fired. It wasn't hard. In fact, it disappointed him that it was so easy. All he had to do was make it look as if she had stolen a piece of jewelry from his mother's jewelry box. The nanny had denied it, but Theo said he had seen her do it, expressing sadness that he had to tell on her.

It was his first taste of control. And he loved it. At his father's workspace, he was the ideal adolescent boy learning his father's business. He showed kindness, intelligence, and smiled at all the right times. The women working there fawned all over him. The men wished their sons were more like Theo.

He didn't rebel. He didn't talk back. He hung on every word that they said. He shook hands like a man and didn't chase after girls—the perfect son.

Yes, Theo thought, as he took one last look in the mirror, the perfect son for a cold-hearted bitch of a mother, and a vacant—and in Theo's eyes—stupid father. Neither of them had seen past the front he had put on since overhearing the nanny. His mother didn't notice because she didn't care. She just wanted her wealth, a husband who didn't embarrass her by flaunting his outside activities, and a son who didn't bother her.

The only thing she had said about his wedding to Edith Warren was that she wasn't good enough for him. Why not marry a rich girl?

If he had answered her instead of walking away, Theo would have said he didn't need a rich girl. He could make all the money he wanted.

What he needed was the perfect wife. The woman all men lusted over, but could never have because she was a principled woman. The woman who would give him the child he needed to prove his manhood. The woman who would not notice, or if she did not tell, his own outside activities.

Activities so much worse than his father's. His father's affairs paled in comparison to what he had already begun to do.

Yes, he needed a wife, just like Edith, to be the perfect front for what would only look like the perfect boring and safe life.

And she would be. Today he would marry her in front of all his parent's friends, and after that, he would own her. He would give her all the love and attention she craved for a few months.

Well, not really, Theo thought. But he knew how to make it look that way. He had wanted a short courtship and fast wedding because he knew he couldn't keep it up for long.

The first day he had seen Edith in the H.U.B. on campus, he knew she was the one. All the men stared at her shining dark hair, sparkling blue eyes, round-in-all-the-right places body, and wished she was theirs. But what made her perfect was the women liked her too. She made friends wherever she went. She was the ideal wife.

But her friend Connie, that was another story. He knew Connie didn't like him. Somehow she had seen past the facade. But that excited Theo. Connie's wiry thin body and ambition made her much more attractive to him. She was dangerous, and that meant he needed to control her. He liked that he needed to rein her in, and he knew exactly how he planned to do it.

However, in the past month, Connie had changed, become warier of him. He saw her flinch when he came near. He didn't know what that was about, but after he finished with her, she wouldn't be flinching anymore. She would be too scared.

His excitement made his face flush, bringing an even healthier look to his complexion. Yes, he would look the part of the perfect groom. A prince. Theo loved that his last name was Prince. So ironic. Yes, he was a prince of a man.

Theo heard a soft knock on the hotel room door and knew that it was Edith's queer brother, Bill. He didn't know why others didn't see it, but it gave him leverage because he did.

Theo also knew that Bill didn't like him; he just pretended to. Theo had seen how Connie and Bill whispered together, and he knew some of it was about him.

He might have to do something about Bill, too. Maybe the same thing he would do to Connie, although doing that to a man would be a novel experience. Perhaps a pleasant one.

He'd have to try it out. But not now. For now, he would be the perfect groom, and his best man, Bill Warren, was waiting to take him to the church.

Theo was ready to begin his perfectly planned life, and no one could stop him.

FORTY

Eddie hovered about the ceremony. He wasn't sure it was the wisest thing he had ever done, but the compulsion to see the event made him break his own rule of not getting too emotionally involved with a mission.

How could he not be emotionally involved? He had resulted from this union. He needed to see all the pieces of it. Of course, he had not been there the first time. It was strange, even to him, that he was here now.

His father was standing at the altar, waiting for his mother to walk down the aisle. Standing beside his father was his Uncle Bill. Standing beside Bill were some of his father's friends from school.

Eddie knew that his father would never speak to any of them again. They had nothing to offer him. He had gotten what he wanted. He had only acquired them so he could appear to be the perfect frat boy, the ideal student. Now that school was over, Theo would become the perfect businessman. On the surface. As always.

When he was alive, Eddie had never seen both sets of grandparents together. Not that Lorraine and Ralph hadn't tried to get together with his father's family. But Virginia and Joseph would never lower themselves to come to Doveland and visit that tiny hovel, as they called it. It would mortify them, or so they said.

Eddie knew that there was more to it than that. He knew Virginia and Joseph didn't want anyone to get close enough to see what was really going on. The cracks in the facade. The lies about their lives.

Even now, so many years later and so many lessons in gratitude and humility, Eddie still felt angry at what had happened.

But he couldn't let it take over his thinking. Because if he did, Connie wouldn't succeed, and he would not get to leave the in-between. But more than that, he refused to let down his mother.

Eddie drifted over to sit beside Lorraine. He laid his head on his grandmother's shoulder and held her hand. She smiled. That she didn't even know him yet, and he was only a spirit watching her now, and still she smiled, made him want to weep knowing what was to come. His beloved grandparents would die of broken hearts.

He sighed and straightened himself. He had work to do, and they would all reunite if he and his little team of Connie, Bryan, and Rachel pulled this mission off.

The wedding was beautiful. Although Edith ended up in the expensive dress that Virginia had insisted on, it fit her perfectly, and she looked stunning as she walked down the aisle on her father's arm. Both Lorraine and Ralph were beaming.

Eddie thought Connie looked beautiful too. It was interesting to see her as a youthful woman. He had never met her when he was alive. He only saw pictures of her that his mother kept in her purse. Theo didn't believe photos of Edith's family, or past friends, belonged in their home.

But even though this was Connie, it wasn't the Connie from the past. It was Connie from the future, the one who knew things.

So although she was smiling and looking at Edith with love,

there was a hardness in her eyes when she looked at Theo. She forced herself to look away, and in doing so, saw Eddie sitting beside Lorraine, and stumbled.

Righting herself, Connie smiled. Eddie knew that she was not just smiling at Lorraine but also at him, and a little of the anger he felt faded away. He nodded at her, and she nodded back—both of them acknowledging why they were there.

Eddie watched as his parents exchanged vows and became husband and wife. This had to be the last time he could come directly into the past. From now on, what happened was not something he wanted to see. Besides, he might try to stop it somehow, and that would be disastrous.

Before leaving, Eddie found Connie standing alone outside watching the newly married couple get their pictures taken. Those pictures would only ever be seen in Lorraine and Ralph's house. He remembered staring at them, thinking how beautiful his parents were. Now here they were, in the past, and he was watching them take the pictures he had stared so long at as a child.

Eddie stood beside Connie and whispered that she was doing an impressive job being present in the past. He whispered because he could see other in-betweeners, drifting through the crowd. Some of them even nodded at him, as if they knew him. There were always people like this in gatherings of all kinds.

They would wander through looking for people they knew. Some of them could not accept that they had died and would get frustrated, angry, or break down in tears when no one answered them.

Others refused to leave, looking for loved ones, or waiting for them, or the violence of their death still bound them to the physical realm.

Not everyone had someone like Eddie to assist them. He used to try to help them all but had learned to let it be. He couldn't help everyone.

Connie only saw Eddie, at least for now. Edith and Jillyan thought seeing others in the in-between would be too distracting, so they had blocked that part of her vision. She hadn't seen them when she was alive, so there was no reason to have her deal with them now.

Connie whispered back, "Thank you. But this is so much harder than I thought it would be. I am so angry now, and I wasn't then. Back then, I was just disappointed that Edith had chosen Theo. If I had known then what I know now, I would have tried to stop it."

"Well, you couldn't have stopped it then, either. This would have played out the way it had to. And must now, too. You know that, right?"

Connie nodded. Bill glanced her way and came over and put his arm around her waist.

"Talking to yourself, Connie?" he asked.

Connie waited for a beat, listening as Eddie said goodbye and touched her hand. It surprised her that she could feel it. But technically both of them were dead, so that must have been why.

"Yes, I guess I am," she finally answered, looking up at Bill.

This time around, she loved him even more than she had the first time. *Hindsight could do that,* she thought. This time she could see clearly that Bill was a kind, generous, and brave man. He had stood by her after what happened, and even when she pushed him away, he kept trying to help.

"I was thinking about how beautiful Edith looks."

"And you were also thinking that you don't trust Theo, weren't you?" Bill added under his breath.

Surprised, Connie turned to look at Bill.

"You see it too, don't you?"

When Bill nodded yes, she backed up into his arms, and they stood there together. Her head resting just below his shoulder. They could have been the perfect couple. But it was not meant to be. She knew that then, but she never told him enough how she felt about him.

"Bill," Connie said, turning to face him again, "I meant it when I said that I love you."

"I love you too, Connie," Bill said, leaning down and kissing her on the forehead.

Then both of them turned back to watch the gathering of people, waiting to get their picture taken, both afraid for Edith.

But it was more than that for Connie. She knew this was the beginning of a nightmare. She hoped she had enough courage this time.

Not to stop it. That she couldn't do. But to stay in it.

FORTY ONE

"Are you ready to work now?" Eddie asked Bryan.

When Eddie returned from his parent's wedding, he found Rachel and Bryan walking in the woods. Eddie had watched as they stopped to look up through the branches of the apple tree, and Rachel pulled a branch down so she could better see the small bud of the future apple.

Bryan and Rachel had looked so happy and peaceful that Eddie almost hated to break it up. But he did, giving them a few minutes to get back to the house.

Bryan shook his head and said, "I don't know. I've barely done anything with Connie this past month. I check in with her every night, but sometimes she barely acknowledges me."

Rachel returned with coffee, put her hand on Bryan's arm, and smiled at Eddie.

She had spent the last month learning more about guides and angels. She had asked Grace and her friends what they knew and grilled Bryan about what he was experiencing when he was out of his body and helping people. She wanted to know how many people were around her she couldn't see, and no one was giving her a straightforward answer, so she had looked forward to talking to Eddie about it.

"Before you tell us what is happening next, could I ask you about guides?"

Eddie had been expecting this. Maybe hoping for it. Hoping that Rachel would step into her reason for being part of this mission. She provided grounding for Bryan, but not just for him. Yes, his mother and Jillyan had asked Eddie to help Connie, but they also asked him to help Bryan and Rachel. Bringing them together for this mission was one way to help them both find their work in this lifetime.

And Rachel's work was not just with Bryan. It was also for many of the guides and spirits that needed someone to work with in the physical plane. She could do that for them. So, although he pretended to be annoyed that Rachel asked, he wasn't.

"I mean, how many kinds of guides are there? How do they work? Are there different kinds? Eddie, you are a guide for people in the in-between. Bryan is helping people who live in this physical world by going out of his body. Is that considered a spirit guide, an angel?

"I thought spirit guides were beings that lived in the spirit world that helped us. Not people like Bryan who live in the physical world too.

"And what am I? Am I doing anything useful other than being here for Bryan? Not that I don't want to be here for him. I just feel as if I could be more in life. Like I have more to do, and somehow I am missing it."

Rachel had to keep reminding herself to keep her hand on Bryan's arm because if she unconsciously gestured with it, she would find herself talking to empty space. She wanted to fix her hair, to pull it back off her face, but she needed two hands to do it. Instead, she waited, her green eyes flashing, for Eddie's response.

"It's not a simple answer, Rachel. Everyone calls all the beings that they can't see by a variety of names, like ghosts, angels, spirits, spirit guides, and entities. How they are seen and what we call them is always based on the belief system of the person looking at them.

"But yes, they exist, and they have jobs, missions, and purposes, just as you do. You have a job or work that you do every day. You can see it as a job, or you can see it as a mission.

"Everyone in the physical dimensions has a purpose, a mission. The tool they use to accomplish it doesn't matter. Your mission, Rachel, is to help ground yourself and others in the heart space of love. You are doing it with Bryan, and whether or not you know it, you do it with your friends and the people you help find homes in your real estate business. You also do that for some of the invisible people around you.

"So yes, there are invisible people. Some are living in the in-between. Some are spirits who keep a connection with those in the physical planes who are able to see them. Some assist others in need. It's easiest to understand if you first accept that there are infinite dimensions, many filled with beings just like in this physical dimension you call Earth.

"They are doing their jobs, just as you do yours. You can call them what you wish. But yes, before you ask, even what we are calling physical beings are not. Think of it as a state of mind that thinks it is physical and has things it has to learn to move on.

"Some people are more aware of that than others. Some people, like your new friends, can communicate with them. Like Bryan—and now you through him.

"Which brings us back to what we are doing here. We are helping Connie. She didn't complete her mission during her physical presence on Earth, and now she has a chance for redemption. And in doing so, she will release others to live out their lives more fully. Like her daughter, Karla."

"And you, Eddie," Rachel said.

"And me," Eddie agreed. "If all goes well, that is."

Bryan had listened to the exchange between Rachel and Eddie with growing apprehension. From a dishwasher to this?

Eddie shook his head at Bryan.

"I know you think being a dishwasher and a spirit guide are worlds apart. And that's where you and so many of you physical beings get it all wrong. They are not exclusive. Your mission and purpose have nothing to do with what you do. One 'job' is not more important than another. But thinking it is blocks people from fulfilling the purpose they have. So you are better off than someone who still believes that their job is the purpose of their life.

"That's enough talk. Let me go back to my first question. Are you ready to get to work? Connie has just a brief time until the world turns upside down for her, and I need you to be ready."

FORTY TWO

While Theo and Edith went off on their honeymoon, Connie moved to Pittsburgh to start her new job. She saw it as the stepping stone to the career that she envisioned for herself. A future where someday she would own her own company.

Other than the Warren family, no one else knew her dream, and she understood she had an uphill battle to make it happen. Not because she wasn't capable. She was. It was because she was a woman, and what women were expected to do was exactly what Edith had done.

But not Connie. She had accepted the job in Pittsburgh with a large accounting firm because she wanted to learn the basics of business, and Connie figured she might as well get paid for it while she learned.

Her time with Ralph had prepared her well, so she wasn't worried about how well she would do at work. She was excited about having her own apartment, meaningful work, and the bustle of a city that was in the process of reinventing itself, just like her. She could relate. Besides, Bill worked in the city too, and she looked forward to spending time with him.

But this time, as Connie prepared for her new life, she knew what would happen, and none of it would be what she had envisioned. Not one piece of it. So as she walked through this part of her life again, she felt as if she was watching a nightmare unfold.

The first time around, she was on cloud nine. Every part of her dream was coming true. Ralph and Lorraine had put down the first and last month's rent on a small but sunny apartment and loaned her enough money to buy a used car.

She remembered, and tried to re-create, the excitement of being handed the keys to an almost new blue Pontiac LeMans. A salesman had driven it for a few weeks, and Ralph knew the owner of the dealership, so they gave her a deal on the car. She had loved that car. It represented freedom. Loving it again was easy.

She and Bill shopped for things that would make an enormous difference in her new apartment. Her love of design flared into being, and she decided that the company she would end up running would be about design. It was hard to find the things she wanted to buy at a price she could afford, and that sparked an idea for making inexpensive but well-designed furniture.

This second time around, she tried to remain excited about the idea again, but she knew that not only would she never do that, but it had been a superb idea and done well by companies like IKEA. Not her. Connie added it to her list of things she regretted not doing.

Connie tried to keep the conversations with Bill as close to the original ones as possible. Once in a while, she would say something that made Bill look at her with curiosity, and more than once, he asked her if she was feeling all right.

"Of course! I am just overly excited" she would answer, because at this time in the past, she had been happier with her life than she had ever been.

Now, in this repeat of the past, she was more afraid than she could ever imagine she would be, because underlying everything she said and did was the grim shadow of knowledge about what was coming. And each day brought it closer.

She relied on Bryan more and more each day to keep her sane. Bryan no longer checked in only at night. He came to see her at least three times a day. Sometimes more.

Sometimes she called out to him to help her, but most of the time, her habit of hiding and not asking for help kept her from reaching out, and she would feel a flood of gratitude that Bryan knew she needed him even when she didn't call.

As the day she dreaded got closer, Bryan did his best to remind her that she would survive. But Connie's terror sometimes overwhelmed him, and he would feel helpless himself.

That's when Rachel would tug on the lifeline between them and reel him back to her and life in the present. He would ground himself, and then sometimes immediately return to Connie.

Bryan spent much of his time in the woods, gathering strength from the creatures of the forest. He learned that he could be with Connie and walk at the same time. He wasn't sure that he could interact with other people, though, so he stayed by himself or with Rachel.

The more Bryan worked with Connie, the more often he would see other beings that lived in the in-between and the spirit world. He stayed clear of them as much as possible, trying not to bring attention to himself. Not just because he had a job to do and didn't want to be distracted, but also because Eddie had warned him that just as in the physical dimensions, not everyone was safe to be around.

But he also witnessed things he would never forget. Like the day he saw a group of Native Americans racing through the woods. Eddie had told him that might happen. He might begin to see overlapping times. It took a few minutes for Bryan to register what was happening.

Before he figured it out, he had stood there wondering if he should run. Afterward, he couldn't stop thinking about it. All of this was happening at the same time. How was that possible? Bryan didn't think he would have an answer to that any time soon. Maybe never.

Even though Rachel had not cleared it with Eddie, she told Grace and the Monday night group what was going on with Connie. Not everything. Just enough so they knew that she might need their help if she couldn't reach Bryan on her own.

She had learned that Ava and Johnny would help with that part, while everyone else would support them. Everyone had their roles to play. For the first time in her life, Rachel felt as if she belonged and doing what she was supposed to do. Or, more accurately, as Grace reminded her, she was living her life as herself.

Rachel treasured every word Eddie said about what she was. It was as if by helping Connie and Bryan, a light had turned on in her world, and a fire had kindled in her heart. She was sure she would need this newfound sense of self.

Although she didn't know exactly what would happen to Connie, she had an inkling what it was. After all, Eddie had said that if she didn't go through with it, she wouldn't have Karla. That seemed pretty clear.

What Rachel didn't know was who or how bad it would be. All she knew was if she was this afraid of what would happen, and she was this far removed from it, Connie must be living a nightmare.

FORTY THREE

Ace slept in. He didn't think that he had. When he rolled over in bed to check the time, he thought only a few hours had passed. When he saw the time and glimpsed sunlight through the slit between the curtains, he bolted out of bed, swearing under his breath.

He slipped on his pants and, without bothering to put his shoes on, stepped outside to see if he could see Leo's car. At first, he didn't, so he walked into the parking lot, shielding his eyes from the blazing sun. He heaved a sigh of relief when he saw that the car was still there.

You're an idiot, he mumbled to himself as he walked back to his room, only to find the door closed and, of course, locked.

Leaning his forehead on the door frame, he swore at himself and then remembered that he had left one key in his pants pocket the night before when he had gone out to get a soda and snacks from the vending machine.

At the time, he had berated himself for eating junk food for dinner again, but now he was momentarily grateful for his careless ways.

And that's what I am being, Ace said to himself. *Careless. I shouldn't have let myself sleep in.*

What if Leo had figured out that Alice was in Doveland and gone there already? What if, after rushing all this way to help Alice, he had been sleeping when she needed help?

Ace knew he had to calm himself down and get on with his plan. It didn't matter it was late in the morning, Leo was still at the motel, and it seemed that Leo would wait for him to make the next move.

Yes, he knew that Leo had put a tracker on his car. How else had he ended up being in the same place? It was a game of cat and mouse that they were playing. He was the mouse. But mice often outwitted the cat, and that was precisely what he was going to do.

After a hot shower, followed by a blast of cold water for thirty seconds to wake him up, Ace stood in front of the foggy pealing mirror and did his best to give himself a clean shave. He needed a haircut, and he needed more sleep, but it was the best he could do.

He would see Alice today. But he wasn't planning on driving to Doveland. He had seen a bike shop in town, and that was how he'd get there. He'd leave the room looking as if he was coming back.

Ace knew that somehow Leo would get in the room to make sure that Ace hadn't left. He doubted it would fool Leo for long, but all he needed was time to warn Alice and tell her he was on her side.

Because that was it. He was on her side. He was done with this shady stuff that Leo was into. Ace knew that in choosing sides, he was putting himself at risk. Not only would Leo want to get rid of him, but any of his clients that would find out about it would join Leo in that desire.

Ace didn't fool himself into thinking he would get the girl and live happily ever after. He planned on turning himself in and convincing Alice to go into witness protection with him. He doubted she would do that, but Ace was sure he had enough information that he could make that deal. But first, he needed

Alice.

A few minutes later, Ace was on his way to the bike shop. He had made sure no one saw him leave the room wearing a hat and sunglasses. Walking behind buildings wherever he could in case Leo was watching the road, Ace moved as quickly as he could toward town. The sooner he was heading to Doveland, the better he would feel.

Rounding the last corner, he could see the bike shop across the road. He looked both ways before crossing, took a few steps, and then backed up. A woman was standing outside the Dairy Queen with flaming red hair. She was looking the other way, but how many people had hair like that?

Ace's heart raced. He could talk to her now. All he had to do was figure out a way not to scare her before he had a chance to explain himself.

But then Ace saw what Alice was looking at. Not what, who. Leo saw Ace at the same moment that Ace saw him, which caused both of them to hesitate.

Evie looked behind her to see what her father was looking at, saw Ace, and without thinking, started running. She had no idea where to run to, and if she had been thinking, she would have taken her bike. But there was no time.

All she could think of was, get away from these two men.

She knew who they were. She barely registered that since she knew who they were, her memory had returned, and along with it, the memory of why she had been hiding.

She had something that they wanted, and now she remembered what it was and why she had been going to her grandfather's.

She had decided that she had nowhere else to turn. Her mother had told her stories of what her grandfather did for a living and how kind and smart he was.

Evie remembered asking her mother why she had run away. Her mother said she had chosen the wrong path and ended up with her father, and she never wanted Leo to know who her father was or how to find him.

"Why?" little Alice had asked.

Her mother hadn't answered. Maybe one day she would have told her, but she never had a chance. Because as she ran, Evie remembered the most terrible thing of all.

Her father had killed her mother, so she could tell no one what she knew. But her father wasn't as smart as he thought. Maggie had hidden the information where she knew that her grown-up daughter would eventually find it. And she had.

FORTY FOUR

As Connie drove Edith back into the city, she struggled to keep her actions and thoughts the same as they had been the first time. Edith bounced back and forth from being ecstatic that she was pregnant and worried about what Theo would say.

Connie could tell her truthfully that Theo would be delighted—because he was. At first. Having children was one of the primary reasons why he had married. He needed an heir. He needed a family. Even then, Connie had suspected that was a front. Now she knew exactly what he had been doing.

Since the first time around, she hadn't known—she had only suspected—it was easy to assure Connie that a baby was what Theo wanted. Before leaving Doveland, Edith had called Theo and told him they were on the way home, and she had a surprise for him. He told her he couldn't wait to see it.

Edith had laughed, and then after hanging up, whispered to Connie that it would be eight months before he could see it.

Connie nodded, thinking, yes, eight long months. But at that moment, it had been a light-hearted exchange between two friends.

That morning around the kitchen table, they had giggled

together and then had one of Lorraine's famous pancake breakfasts. Lorraine and Ralph beamed at everything that Edith said. Edith was giving them a grandchild.

"What could be more glorious than a new child coming into our family," they had said, hugging the two of them goodbye.

Both girls promised they would visit again soon. Only one of them knew she wouldn't come back.

Edith insisted that Connie come into the house while she told Theo. She wanted Connie to share the moment with her.

Connie knew that Edith would keep that memory locked up inside her for the rest of her life. Taking it out from time to time to look at it, treasure it, and then ask herself, "What did I do wrong?"

Seeing Theo, and remembering the pain he caused, Connie wanted to reach out and slap him across the face, throw him to the ground, and stomp on him. Not that she physically could have done that. It was what she wanted to do. Instead, she had clapped and laughed as Edith told Theo.

She watched Theo even more closely than she had last time. She saw the flash of anger at the news, and then it changed to the perfect expression of happiness at hearing he would be a father. He hugged Edith, lifting her and turning with her around and around, telling her how happy he was.

Connie braced herself, knowing what would come next. Theo hugged her too and then holding her by the shoulders suggested that she stay the night, and they could continue to celebrate. It took all of Connie's self-control to nod with a smile on her face and say that it would delight her to stay.

Although parts of the house were still being worked on, the guest room was ready. Edith walked Connie upstairs with her things and opened the door to the room with a flourish.

"I asked to have it done in your favorite colors," Edith said. "I wanted it to be a surprise for you. It's your room. You can come and stay anytime. Theo loved the idea too. He said you're like a sister to him."

Connie had laughed then as she laughed now. The room was beautiful, shades of blue, with accents of lavender and white. She had sighed with happiness the first time she saw it. She had thought yes, perhaps she could spend some happy hours here with Edith and Theo. She could learn to like him, if only for Edith and the new baby's sake.

If Theo had not been who he was, or at least not brought it into his own home, perhaps life could have developed that way.

Mentally, Connie shook her head. She already knew the terrible thing that would happen. She had lived through it before. She could do it again.

Before going to dinner, Connie sat on the blue and white plaid chair by the window that overlooked the most manicured garden she had ever seen and called Bryan. He answered right away. When she could feel his presence, she asked him to be present physically too.

Bryan had done that a few times, but he was still learning the skill, so although he appeared in front of her, she had to look closely to see him.

"What do you need?" Bryan asked.

"I don't know," Connie answered. "What can you do? I have to let this happen. But if I know that you and Rachel are with me, it might be easier. But I am also embarrassed. How can I ask this of you?"

Bryan sat in the other chair in the room. The one by the bed and said, "I'll be here. I'll be a witness to your bravery."

Connie smiled at Bryan through her tears. She stepped to the mirror and ran her hands through her hair, making it stick up just a bit, the way she liked it. The sun had tipped the ends, and Connie knew that she had never looked more beautiful than she had this night. Maybe if she did it all right this time, she would feel beautiful again someday.

So that night at dinner, Connie let herself watch what she knew Theo would do. She watched him drop something into her drink.

She hadn't seen it before. This time she had, and yet she picked up that drink, smiled, and toasted to Edith and the baby that was coming as if there was no evil in the room, grinning at the two of them, shining through Theo's eyes.

She said what she had said before, "Wow, I must have drunk more than I thought."

She let Edith help her up to her room and tuck her into bed while telling her how happy she was, and she would see Connie in the morning.

She lay there, knowing she still had time. She could call for help. She could stumble down the stairs and drive at least a few blocks away, thwarting what would come next.

She did none of those things. This was not the place where she had to change things. This was what she had to go through again.

So she lay in bed as the paralysis took over. Felt the same terror. Actually, she felt more terror because she knew what would happen next.

She heard the slight squeak of the door, and Theo mumble to himself to get someone to take care of that. She opened her eyes as she had the last time. Eyes filled with fear and terror, and finally sorrow for herself, as Theo brutally raped her over and over again. She knew that in the morning, she would find bruises over her entire body, where no one could see them.

She kept her eyes open this time as dawn broke, and Theo leaned over her and said if she told anyone, he would kill Edith's baby.

"Do you understand? Blink if you do."

She blinked.

"I'll tell Edith that you don't feel well and are staying in bed this morning. Then take a shower, get dressed, and leave this house and never come back. Or I'll do this again. Blink again if you understand."

Connie blinked.

Yes, that's what she did the last time. She never came back. This time she would.

FORTY FIVE

Connie called in sick that day. And the next. It was what she had done before, and it was easy to repeat. She had no desire to change anything. Yet.

Bill called and asked how the trip went, and she mumbled that she was sick and hung up on him.

The first time it had happened, she went through the stages of denial, rage, grief. This time, each stage was even more intense because Connie knew the consequences of Theo's brutality, one of which was her daughter, Karla.

In a month, she would go to the doctor and find out she was pregnant. She would drag herself through the next weeks in a state of confusion that bordered on insanity.

Her work would suffer, and her employers would warn her she wasn't living up to their expectations. She would alternate between hatred and awe.

The first time, she had contemplated having an abortion. Her life was just beginning. She had plans. Having a child would change everything. The child was the product of violence. But it wasn't only the fact that abortions were both illegal and dangerous in 1968 that stopped her then. It was the feeling of love for a child she didn't know yet.

That was then. Now, Connie of the future knew even more about why she wanted the child.

Karla had turned out to be everything anyone would want from a daughter. Kind, generous, intelligent, and witty. And sad. But that wasn't Karla's fault. It was hers. It was because of what Connie had done with her life that took away Karla's happiness. Theo may have started the problem, but it was what she did afterward that ruined so many lives.

In the past, Connie only had to deal with what had happened to her. Now she had to deal with what she knew would happen. Connie knew that she had to figure out at what point she would change the past. There were so many small decisions that she had made.

Which choice was the one that would tip the future into one that brought Karla joy, not sadness? Which one would release her from the in-between? Which decision would help Eddie? Would he still die? If he didn't die, how could he have helped her in a future where he hadn't died?

Perhaps he wouldn't have had to help her because she wouldn't have ended up in the in-between. Maybe she would have lived longer.

Connie had no answers to all her questions. So besides reacting to what had happened to her then, and what she knew was coming, Connie felt even more insane than she had the first time.

Eddie had warned her about feeling this way, but he hadn't given her any answers to make it better either. All her decisions had to be hers and hers alone. It had been hard then. Now it tore her apart. With that one act, Theo did what he wanted to do. Destroy the future for her and everyone she loved.

• • ● ● ● ● ● • •

Connie was not the only one suffering from that act. Bryan had returned from that evening filled with rage.

It was a rage so deep it made him want to go out into the streets and scream. Maybe throw rocks through a window, find someone, and beat them to a pulp.

It terrified him that he felt that way. Was he a violent person? Could he actually do those things he felt like doing?

Bryan had always seen himself as a gentle person. Maybe too passive, but not violent. The rabbits on his walk seemed like tiny versions of himself. Peaceful. A little playful. But perhaps useless in the big scheme of things.

Now Bryan felt more like a wild dog, ready to rip into anyone and anything that crossed his path. Including Rachel.

She had pulled him back and then stepped away. She had suspected that was what would happen, so was prepared for how upset Bryan might be. But he was far angrier than she had expected.

Although he didn't tell her any details—she didn't really want to know them—she guessed it had been terrible. He had hissed at her to leave him alone and then went into his room and slammed the door.

If he had let her, she would have put her arms around him and held him, which would have helped her too. But he left her to deal with her feelings on her own. Except she decided she didn't need to do it alone. She had friends who could help.

When Bryan didn't come out of his room, she left him a note saying she was going to the coffee shop, and please call when he was ready to talk.

One of the many reasons Rachel had always loved living in

Doveland was that most of what she wanted in town was within walking distance.

But instead of walking straight to the coffee shop, she made a detour and passed by Edith's family home. She didn't know what she expected to find. Perhaps some answers. Or a feeling about what to do to help Bryan and Connie. Rachel couldn't imagine how difficult it would be to return to a past that was so horrific, let it happen, and then deal with the consequences and the ramifications of what it would do to the future.

Rachel worried about Connie. What if Connie chose the wrong thing and what happened after that was worse than before? Or perhaps Connie's life improved, but would everyone's get better? How many things would change based on what Connie did?

Standing in front of Edith's old home, Rachel thought the house looked a little different from the last time she had been there. Maybe it was her imagination. Or was it part of what was going on for Connie in the past?

Rachel sighed and turned away. She needed to talk to someone. A few minutes later, Grace looked up as Rachel slipped into a booth along the wall, and without thinking twice, gave Valerie a call and asked her if she could come over. Grace would have called Barbara, but she knew that Pete and Barb would be in the middle of the breakfast rush at the Diner.

A few minutes later, Valerie slid into the booth across from Rachel, and Grace slid in next to her. Rachel attempted to smile at them both but managed only a weak version of her usual smile.

Grace reached over to grab Rachel's hands and said, "Okay, dear. We'll listen. You talk."

An hour later, Rachel stood, gave Grace and Valerie hugs, and headed back to Bryan's. She would insist on doing the same thing for Bryan. She would listen. He would talk. And together, they would figure out how to help Connie.

FORTY SIX

"This is my last visit," Eddie said.

Connie cried. They were in her apartment in Pittsburgh, so different from the first time she had seen him waiting for her in her garden. She missed that garden and wondered if she would end up in it again someday.

"If things go well," Eddie answered her unspoken thought.

Back at her house, Connie had resisted Eddie. Well, she had resisted everything. That she had died was at the top of the list. Now she wanted to hug Eddie and thank him for giving her a second chance. But she couldn't. Now she was a physical body in the past, and he was still a spirit guide in the in-between.

"Will I ever see you again?" Connie asked, crying silently. Her emotions were all over the place these days for more than one reason. In the past, she would have tried to hide her feelings. Now she let herself be present with them, knowing that not expressing them before had helped bring about the life she had lived. She would not repeat that mistake.

"If things go well," Eddie said again. He paused before continuing, Connie's tears making him want to cry too.

"But not in the same way. You have help now. Bryan and Rachel will also have help in case they run into trouble."

"What if I don't make the right choices?" Connie asked. "What then? Maybe things will be worse, and I never see you again. So many terrible things could happen."

"And so many marvelous things could happen, too," Eddie said, reaching out to hold Connie's hand. For a moment, Connie thought she could feel his touch, and then he was gone.

She let herself cry. Then she rose, stretched, glimpsed the wreck of herself in the mirror, and made a decision. She needed to see Bill. She phoned his office and made an appointment for that morning.

Bill laughed and said she didn't need an appointment. She told him that what she needed to talk to him about required an appointment and hung up before he could say anything.

She took a shower, chose clothes that made her feel put together, added a little makeup, and ate a piece of dry toast, the only thing she could keep down these days.

Before leaving her apartment, she checked the mirror. There were dark circles under her eyes, and she looked as if she had been sick, but at least it wasn't the ghastly wreck she had seen a few hours before.

Bill was waiting for her at the elevator. He took one look at her and said, "We are not meeting here. I don't know what's going on, but you will tell me everything."

They walked to a Denny's near Bill's office, and Bill chose a booth tucked away in the back corner of the restaurant. After the waitress filled their coffee cups, Bill leaned forward and said, "Talk to me."

Connie stared at her cup, contemplating the possible results of telling Bill. She had not told him the first time. She had slunk away to the trailer park and told Mama Woo what happened. That's when she had learned that her father had died a few years before—dropped dead in an alley behind a bar where he had drunk himself to death every night of his adult life. She had not cried. She only felt relieved knowing that she wouldn't see him again.

After weeping and swearing about the situation, Mama Woo took over. She and the other women arranged for Connie to stay with them in a trailer that had stood empty for six months. First, they cleaned it, painted it, and then helped her move from her apartment.

Connie became a member of the trailer park community. It felt familiar, and she felt safe. No one knew about it. King's Row had been her secret, and once again it became her home.

She had quit the job she had worked so hard to get, told Edith that she had to go away for a while, and disconnected her phone. Bill and his family had no idea where she had gone. She had broken their hearts, along with her own. But at the time, she thought she was saving Edith and her baby. That turned out not to be true. But she hadn't really known Theo then.

While living in the park, Connie got a job at a local furniture shop, and it turned out to be the best thing to have happened to her. She was so good at helping people pick out furniture that they asked her for more advice, and she started what eventually grew into her design consulting business.

The job, and her own business, kept her busy during her pregnancy. After Karla was born, she didn't return to the furniture store. She worked out of the trailer, and she grew her business enough to keep herself and Karla fed and sheltered.

But when Karla turned two, Mama Woo said they had to move on. Find some place else to live. Make a life that meant something. Mama Woo said that Connie hadn't worked as hard as she had to end up like them. She pushed and prodded Connie, asking her where her gumption had gone.

Finally, she and the women simply locked the trailer and wouldn't let Connie back in. All her belongings were in the tiny yard, and one of the women had Karla in her trailer, packed and ready to go.

Connie had been furious. She screamed and yelled until she finally broke down and hugged every woman as if she would never see them again. She told them that they were her family, and she would never forget them. And despite everything else that she didn't do right in her life, she returned as often as possible to see them.

That day they helped her put all her belongings in the Pontiac, and after hugging everyone again, and with all of them crying, she and Karla had driven off.

Mama Woo had given Connie the name of a woman she had once known who she thought could help Connie make a home in another small town near Pittsburgh, and Connie wisely accepted the help that the woman offered.

And that was where she had lived out the rest of her days, eventually buying the home they had first moved into. She and Karla often visited the park until Mama Woo died, and the other women moved away. Without Mama Woo, the "community" was gone.

That is what she did the last time. This time she was doing something different. This time she would tell Bill. Connie prayed that this was the right thing to do because, after that, everything would change.

FORTY SEVEN

Sitting across from Bill, Connie knew that she had two stories to tell. One was about Theo, and one was that she wasn't who she appeared to be. She had to decide. Would she tell him the second one? Did she have to? If she didn't tell him, how would she convince Bill about Theo?

Because it wasn't just the rape that she had to tell him about, it was what Theo had been hiding all along. Even though in the past, she had hidden from everyone except Mama Woo and the other women of the trailer park, she had not stopped watching over Edith and her family.

Watching over was not an adequate term for it, because she did nothing to keep them safe. She told herself that she couldn't have because it took years to collect information before she realized all that Theo had been doing. She had proof in the future. In the past, the evidence would be hard to find.

Connie felt stuck. She didn't know where to start, and she was terrified about the consequences of her actions. But then Connie reminded herself what the lack of action had produced. She also knew that she couldn't do what needed to be done on her own. She needed help in stopping Theo, and if all went well, saving Edith and Eddie.

Bill sat across from her, waiting, his clear blue eyes filled with compassion. He knew what it was like to be careful about revealing too much, and he could see Connie struggling with what to say. The waitress topped off their coffee and asked if they wanted to order breakfast.

Connie shook her head no, and Bill handed the waitress ten dollars and said, "Thank you, that's all we need."

Watching Bill's kind gesture released Connie from her paralyzed state. At that moment, she realized that Theo had paralyzed her twice. Once with a drug, and again with his words.

No more, she thought to herself.

She began at the beginning—how she had always been worried about Theo. Didn't like him very much, but couldn't figure out why. Bill nodded and said that he had that same feeling.

Encouraged, Connie continued. When she got to the part where Lorraine had figured out that Edith was pregnant, Bill broke out in an enormous smile and said Edith had called him with the news, and he couldn't wait to be an uncle.

Connie waited for a beat, remembering what a good uncle Bill had been to Eddie, and hoped that if this went well, Bill would be an honorary uncle to Karla this time around.

When Connie told Bill about what happened in the guest bedroom at Edith's home, Bill stood, causing the coffee cups to rattle, and hissed, "I will kill that bastard." A few other customers looked their way, and Connie reached out and pulled Bill back into his seat.

"No, you won't. But we do have to stop him."

"Stop him? But he already did it!"

"Yes. But I can't prove it."

Bill hung his head and asked what he could do. Connie thought about how hard it would be to have Theo arrested, even if this had happened in the future.

Now, in the past, it would be impossible. There was no DNA testing. They often accused women of causing the rape to happen. Not much has changed, Connie thought. But in 1968, it was almost always the woman's fault.

Connie realized then that she couldn't tell Bill half the story. She had to tell him the entire thing because she couldn't explain how she knew she was pregnant when only a few days had gone by.

Taking a deep breath, Connie said, "There's more to this, Bill, but I am not sure how to explain it to you. It's entirely possible that you will think that I am crazy. But I do know that Theo does this to many, many women, and eventually kills one, which starts him off on a killing spree."

"How could you possibly know that, Connie? Yes, what he did to you makes him a monster, but you can't know what he does in the future."

"This is where I am afraid you will think I'm crazy."

At that moment, Bryan showed up and sat beside Bill. Bill couldn't see him, but she could, and Bryan knew it. He was there to support her, remind her she wasn't crazy, and that she had a job to do.

"Well, we won't know until you tell me," Bill said, giving her a wan smile. "If you know something that will punish him for what he did to you, and stop him from hurting others, you have to tell me."

Connie leaned back against the red backrest of the booth and took a moment to look around the restaurant. She thought nothing would immediately change once she began, but just in case she wanted to remember how things used to be.

She took a deep breath and said, "I know things, Bill. Because I am not the Connie you knew in 1968. I am a different Connie."

Bill snorted and started laughing. He laughed so hard, his face turned a bright red, but when he noticed that Connie wasn't smiling, he stopped.

"You're not joking? But it is 1968, and you are sitting right there. I know you. We've been friends for years."

Connie sighed. "Yes, I am still Connie, and yes, we have been friends for years. But I am a different Connie. I am a Connie from the future. Quite a distant future, in fact. One where you and I are old. One in which I died."

Connie had whispered that last part. Bill had leaned in to hear her.

Bryan had moved to sit beside Connie, and she appreciated his nearness and took his hand under the table. She could almost feel it. Bryan was becoming more real in this lifetime. She didn't have time to wonder if that was a good thing or not before Bill whispered back, "You're not kidding, are you?"

Connie shook her head, no.

Bill stood, took another five dollars out of his wallet, and smacked it down onto the table.

"Come on, we are getting out of here, and you will do everything you can to convince me you are telling the truth, and you haven't gone crazy."

As Connie followed Bill out of Denny's and into the world, she was happy that everything looked the same. So far, nothing had changed here, except Bill's mood. On the other hand, she had no idea what it had done to the future.

FORTY EIGHT

Rachel felt a shiver as if an icy wind had passed through her. She was once again sitting on the park bench. It was one of those beautiful spring days when everything is right with the world. Every shade of green was the backdrop for the diverse mix of flowers that edged the park walks. Birds sang in the trees, and a light breeze rustled her hair. She had been on her way to the coffee shop when she saw Johnny leaning back on the park bench with his eyes closed, the sun on his face.

Although she had just become friends with Valerie and her sons, Rachel had known about them. You couldn't live in as small a town as Doveland and not know who everyone was, even if you never met.

So she had watched Johnny change the past few years from the boy with piercings and all-black clothes getting into trouble, to this quiet and thoughtful young man.

Rachel knew it was mainly the result of Ava and Grace and their friends directing him down a different path and taking him and his family under their wing. Now she was under their care too. It felt wonderful.

As she sat down beside Johnny, he said, "Hi, Rachel," without opening his eyes. "Something is changing. Can you feel it?"

It was then that she felt the shiver and Johnny sat up, opened his eyes, and said, "Hm. Interesting."

Then, as if he was alone and only talking to himself, he leaned back and closed his eyes again.

Rachel waited for him to say more, and when he didn't, she asked, "What's changing. What's interesting? And since you were waiting for me, what is happening?"

Johnny sat up and turned to Rachel. "Sorry. It's interesting to watch Connie try to prove to her friend Bill that she is from the future. She appears to be succeeding. He's skeptical but willing to trust her, which is changing things. So far, nothing major."

"I don't get how that works," Rachel said.

"No one does, really," Johnny answered. "On our part, it is often trial, and sometimes error. But I think there is something else keeping the changes contained.

"Maybe someone else. I don't know. But I think it has to do with what the intention is that drives the changes. Or maybe we are constantly moving to alternative universes. It's a mystery.

"But I have a belief that it turns out for good. If that was the intent in the first place, and that definitely is Connie's intent. And yours, for that matter."

Seeing Rachel staring at him, Johnny laughed. "Oh. Sorry again. I appear to be stuck between talking too much or not at all.

"Anyway, I wanted to see you to let you know that I am also watching over the situation, so if you or Bryan need help, I'm here."

Rachel looked out over the park and wondered how many worlds, or parallel universes, were going on right where they were, and how many people moved around them that she couldn't see.

"The parallel universe question, I don't know the answer to. But about how many people, I can see about ten of them right now. Sometimes there are more, sometimes less. Mostly they don't see us though, so not to worry."

"Wait, how did you know what I was thinking? Are you doing that all the time? To everyone?"

"Heard you thinking. I am practicing getting better at it. I don't do it all the time. That would be wrong. Only when I am already having a conversation with someone, or need to check in on a situation."

Seeing Rachel's face, he added, "I know it might sound like a marvelous thing, but when I was a kid, it wasn't. I honestly thought I was crazy. So I acted crazy.

"Then I learned from Ava and her friends that it is a gift. And like all gifts, it is sometimes good, sometimes hard, often overwhelming. I struggle not to feel responsible for fixing the things I see. But I now recognize that it is a gift, and one that I am learning to be grateful for."

Rachel nodded. "I've always been the normal person—the one who didn't make waves or ask for what they wanted. So I didn't think I was crazy. I felt like my life was insignificant.

"Since Bryan's mom died and opened that door for him, and then that kid Eddie appeared and told me I would be Bryan's lifeline back to the present and the physical universe, things are entirely different.

"But even when I was normal, or what passes for normal, I still struggled. Maybe everyone does. But now that I am getting a glimpse of my gifts, I worry even more about what I am supposed to do."

"Well," Johnny said, "What works best for me is concentrating on one thing at a time. And trying to remember that I am not in charge."

"So the one thing you are concentrating on right now is what's going on with Connie? Did Grace and your mom ask you to do this?"

"Yes, and yes!" Johnny said. "And that means we get to go to

Pittsburgh and see Bill."

"See Bill?" squeaked Rachel. "Bill is still alive?"

"Of course, he is. And will remain so if we can get the information we need about Theo to the past Connie and Bill as soon as possible. And since Bill is the one still alive, he's the one we'll see. Oh, and you'll be driving, and yes, my mother knows what's happening.'"

Rachel realized there was no point in not doing what Johnny wanted. After all, she was the one who didn't know what was going on. As she stood, she turned to see Grace coming towards them, holding two brown bags.

"I packed you both a lunch, in case you are hungry. You have Bill's address?" Grace asked, addressing Johnny.

"Yep. And the GPS will take us right to his door."

"Wait, shouldn't I tell Bryan where we are going? What if he needs me?"

"We'll both keep tabs on him as we go. I'll watch while you drive."

Grace added, "I'll go see him later and bring him food and let him know what you two are up to."

"Okay, that settles it," Rachel said, heading toward her car parked across the street.

She wondered if she could put all these things together in her head and decided she couldn't. But she could get them to Bill's house, and once they were there, obviously Johnny knew what to do.

"Well, I don't yet," Johnny said, "But I'm working on it. It's what I mean about taking one right step at a time."

Pulling a laptop out of the bag he had been carrying, Johnny added, "Thanks to Dan, our police chief, I have access to files that might help us."

Rachel started to ask why the police chief would give Johnny access to files and then remembered some stories she had heard about Dan working with Ava and Grace in the past. He must know about what they could do.

"Oh, he does," Johnny mumbled as he typed. "Not all of it, but enough to know that helping us is a good thing."

And for the next ninety minutes, Johnny typed and grumbled and talked to himself, as Rachel drove with the soundtrack from *Guardians of the Galaxy* playing in her ear. It kept her thoughts away, which was just what she needed.

As they pulled up in front of Bill's house, Johnny closed his laptop and said, "Excellent choice on the soundtrack. In a way, we are the guardians of this tiny piece of the galaxy."

"Well, if you could hear it the whole time, why couldn't I have played it out loud?"

Johnny laughed. "That would have been too loud. Through your head, it was just right."

Rachel quelled the desire to punch him in the arm and then laughed. This was much more fun than sitting at home alone, wondering what to do with her life.

Johnny linked arms with her as they headed up the walk, "Yes, it is, isn't it?"

Rachel wondered if she would ever get used to him listening in on her thoughts, and as he rang the doorbell, Johnny said, "Probably not."

Rachel had no chance to fume. The door opened, revealing a tall thin man with white hair and very blue eyes.

"I've been expecting you," he said.

FORTY NINE

Rachel and Johnny followed Bill as he shuffle-walked through the hall to his living room. He gestured to the couch and then settled himself into a lounge chair.

A man carrying a tray with four glasses of what Rachel assumed was ice tea came into the room, and Bill introduced him as his husband, Terrance Laing.

Rachel and Johnny said hello to Terrance, and each took a glass.

"You know it's been such a brief time since I could casually introduce Terrance as my husband and have people just as casually acknowledge it, that I brace myself every time. But you aren't here to talk about that, are you? You're here to make sure I do something for Connie."

As Rachel and Johnny exchanged glances, Bill added, "Oh, don't worry, Terrance knows what's going on. He knew Connie then, too. And Connie knew that Terrance and I were together. Even then."

"You've been together that long?" Rachel exclaimed.

"Yes," Terrance answered. "We were young men together, and now we are old men together. It's the together part that makes life worthwhile. So yes, I met Connie a few times. But she left and kept away from all of us not long after I met her, so I barely got to know her."

"And," Bill continued, "We know now that she recently died. But the odd thing is, we didn't know about it until we got a letter from her, saying she died. How can that be?"

Rachel and Johnny waited.

"Anyway, the letter said she had died and that you two would show up. And then I should put what you are bringing me, and the package that arrived with the letter, in my safe in my office. This is quite the mystery, don't you think?" Bill asked with a twinkle in his eye.

Terrance added, "But we are not supposed to ask you what it is all about. We are just supposed to do it."

Rachel and Johnny looked at each other, before Rachel asked, "Are you willing to just do it knowing nothing?"

Bill leaned back and then reached over to hold Terrance's hand.

"When I first met Connie, she looked at me and saw me. She was the first person in my life who had ever done that for me. Not only did she see me, but she didn't think I was strange, or different, or evil. I don't know how she did that, but it was because of her I thought I might survive being me.

"Yes, when I got the courage to tell my parents, they were accepting too. I know now that I should have told them sooner. But I didn't have to tell Connie. She knew. That's how she was. She knew things.

"I don't understand why she left and why she didn't return when Edith and then Eddie died, and then my parents died soon after that. I know she loved my family. So she must have had a good reason for not being there."

Bill brushed tears away. "Sorry, so many years have gone by, and I still can't get over missing them."

He took a deep breath and continued, "But I could have visited her, too. I had a private investigator look for her. Amazingly, she didn't live that far away. But I was a coward. Terrance kept urging me to go, but I was afraid. Afraid it wouldn't be the same Connie, and she wouldn't know me anymore, or worse, reject me.

"So, I stayed away. When I learned that Connie had a daughter, I assumed Connie left because she was pregnant and didn't want us to know.

"It still breaks my heart because we wouldn't have cared that she wasn't married. Now that this mystery thing is happening, I am wondering if there was more than that. Is it something you know? Is it something that you can tell me?"

When neither of them said anything, Bill added, "Please. Tell me why she never came back."

It was Rachel who answered, "It won't unbreak your heart Bill if we told you, but if we can do what Connie has asked of you, perhaps you will know the answer for yourself."

"Putting these papers in my safe will change what happened? That makes little sense. But I don't see how it can hurt."

Terrance looked at Rachel and Johnny and asked, "But it might? Because this will change the past somehow, won't it?"

"Yes," Johnny said, trying not to explain more.

As Bill stood, he asked, "So if it changes the past, wouldn't that change the future? Wouldn't that mean that our lives will be different? How do I know it will be better? I don't want to lose Terrance. Can you promise me we will still be together?"

Rachel and Johnny stood too as Johnny answered the question.

"No, we can't. All I know is that our intentions and Connie's intention in asking you to do this are good. Sometimes that means that things can still go wrong, but if you don't do this, I know that some terrible things happen."

Terrance turned to Bill and said, "It's okay. We've had a wonderful life together. And if by doing this it means we don't, but it will help other people, then you know you have to do it.

"And Connie, bless her heart, knew you well, Bill. She knew you would help her now, as you would have helped her then. But she never asked. After all these years, we have a chance to help her. We can't turn her down now. She trusted you to do the right thing." Bill touched Terrance on the cheek and then turned to Johnny.

"One last question," Bill said, "Why doesn't she want me to see what's in the package?"

Rachel put her hand on Bill's arm, "I think it is because she loved you, and reading this will break your heart even more."

Bill nodded, tears running down his face, and led them into his office. "Is this going to work because this is the same house I have always lived in?"

Johnny shrugged. Bill nodded, "Well, I will pretend that's why, and be grateful that we stayed put."

As Bill put his package in the safe, and Johnny added what he got from Dan, Johnny tried to suppress the fear that rose in him. What if doing this changed who he was, his life, his mother, Rachel? What if he was no longer himself?

None of those questions could be answered, and even if life was different, would he know? For all he knew, they had done this before, and this life was a result.

Too many questions, no answers, just do what you have to do, he said to himself, half expecting the world to shift under his feet as Bill shut the safe and twirled the lock.

FIFTY

"Will you stay with me?" Connie asked Bryan.

Up to now, Bryan had remained, not only as a voice in her head but as a form she could see.

She was grateful that no one else could see him, although she had a brief scare when a little girl on her way out of the restaurant with her mom said, "Hello," and looked straight at Bryan. Bryan had smiled and said hello back.

The girl kept tugging at her mom's hand, keeping her eye on Bryan the whole way to the door. Thankfully, the mom thought her daughter had said hello to Connie and thought nothing of it.

"I need to rest for a minute," Bryan answered, dissolving away. She barely heard the words, "I'll meet you at Bill's," before he was gone.

"Who are you talking to?" Bill asked.

Connie shook her head, "It's not important. Well, it is important, but maybe we should save it until we get to your house?"

"That's where you want to go?" Bill asked.

"That's where we have to go. That is if you want answers."

Connie hoped that the letter and package she had Bryan mail for her had reached the future Bill, and that he was following the instructions in the letter. If not, this Bill would never believe her, and then all of this would be for nothing.

That's when Connie realized something that hadn't occurred to her before. What if, by changing things, Theo decided that it would be best to stop her?

Maybe he became afraid that she would go to the police. In the past, she had left town, and no one knew where she went, including Theo.

This time she had stayed. What if Theo came looking for her? She would be easy to find.

But then Connie reminded herself that it had only been a few days. She had stayed this long before too. Everything was fine. At least for now.

But based on what she had uncovered in the future, Theo had raped another girl only a few days after his assault on her, so if she wanted to stop him this time, she didn't have much time to convince Bill to help her.

• • ● • ● • ● • ● • •

Bryan opened the back gate to his garden, barely walking. He couldn't believe how tired he was. If it hadn't been for the rabbit hopping in front of him, he might have laid down in the path and gone to sleep.

Instead, he followed the white bouncing tail to his home. Even though Bryan didn't think the rabbit did it on purpose, or could hear him, he whispered, "thank you," just in case. The rabbit stopped and looked back, the sun behind him turning his ears a rosy pink.

He could have sworn he heard "You're welcome," but decided that he was probably delirious. Of course, he had just been sitting beside a dead woman who was alive in the past. That was weird enough. Why not a talking rabbit?

Considering how altogether strange his life had become, he wasn't all that surprised to see Grace waiting for him in his back garden.

Briefly, he wondered how she had gotten there, considering that the only way to his garden was through a locked gate or a locked house.

But then he decided it wasn't worth worrying about, especially when she said, "I brought food."

• • • **•** • **•** • • •

Twenty minutes later, Bill and Connie were sitting in Bill's office with Terrance.

Connie had stalled as long as possible by asking for coffee, and then a tour of the house. She hadn't seen it before. Bill had just purchased it and was in the process of upgrading it and designing the interiors.

The kitchen was partially torn apart as was the living room, and despite what they were about to do, Connie couldn't help thinking of what she would do in each room if only Bill would ask her to help. The last time she hadn't had a chance to.

That wasn't his fault. She had run away. This time, if they did what they needed to do, perhaps she would get the chance. At least this time, she wasn't running. On the other hand, if all went well, what was the outcome for her? Would she remain as a person living in the past, but living a different future?

There were so many possible outcomes, and she could control none of them. All she could do now was the right thing. She would do whatever she could to stop Theo before one more person got hurt.

Connie knew she wasn't Theo's first rape. Even then, she had known it. He had planned her rape too well. In the future, she had gathered proof that he had started years before. When they were in college, he had been honing his skill. And she had uncovered that he had actually begun in high school.

However, Theo had been getting into various kinds of trouble long before that. He had hurt animals. He had hurt his friends just for fun. If he got caught and couldn't talk his way out of it, his parents took over. They would blame someone else. Or claim that it was all a mistake. If necessary, they bought his way out of trouble.

But they privately punished him in ways that made it worse. Connie thought, in the beginning, his actions may have been a cry for help. A call no one heard. And then Theo started enjoying himself, and he was lost to the evil ideas that took over in his thoughts.

His parents thought they could stop him by keeping him close. It's why he had gone to Penn State. Like the house they bought for him, it was part of their strategy of containment. But speaking out about it, or allowing others to catch and punish him, was not.

As she researched what Theo was doing and had done, Connie had become more and more enraged. But all she had done was collect evidence. She had done nothing to stop him.

In her own way, she had been just as bad as his parents, maybe worse. All of them had turned a blind eye to what Theo was doing. His parents because they wanted to preserve their reputation, she, because she had become a coward.

Connie had told herself that she wanted to protect her child. She didn't want Theo to know about Karla. He had told her to stay away and keep her mouth shut, and she had obeyed.

Not this time.

FIFTY ONE

N ow, what," Bill said as they settled into his office.

"Now, I need you to open your safe."

Bill shrugged and opened the safe.

"Now, what?" he asked again.

Connie peered over his shoulder and didn't see the package that should have been there, and her heart sank. But she hid her disappointment as she told him to shut the safe, and then they would wait a few minutes and look again.

"What will change in a few minutes?" Terrance asked. "It's a locked safe."

Connie stood and walked to the window, trying to calm herself.

Bill's arm around her broke her resolve, and she struggled not to cry.

"We have to stop Theo. He is an evil, evil man. And I needed the papers that should be in the safe to prove it to you."

"But what papers? How will they get there? While we wait for whatever is supposed to happen, why not tell us everything? Then even if the papers don't show up, we'll know what to do."

"Can you promise me you won't think I'm crazy, Bill? Because this will sound crazy."

"I can promise you we will listen with open minds, and the last person I would ever think was crazy was you. That you are the Connie from the future, yes, that sounds crazy, but stranger things have happened, and personally, I love things that can't easily be explained. I know Terrance does too. So try us, and then we'll look in the safe again in thirty minutes?"

Connie let out a deep sigh and moved to sit down. The two men faced her and taking a deep breath she began.

"In the past, after Theo raped me, I found out I was, am, pregnant."

Bill started to say something, but when Connie held up her hand, he stopped.

"There is too much to this story that will make you want to ask me questions, so just let me tell it the best way that I can first, please."

Both Bill and Terrance nodded their agreement. But Connie could see that both of them were clenching their hands. Connie knew it would get worse, so she plunged ahead.

"In the past, I ran away after the rape. Theo threatened me, and I was a coward. I went to my friends at the trailer park, and they helped me. After my daughter Karla was born, we moved to a small town not that far from here.

"I changed my last name and watched over you and your family. I watched Theo, too. I collected evidence that he was raping and then killing women. But as I said, I was a coward, and I did nothing.

"I know you must be angry at me as I tell you this. I am angry at myself, too. But that's not the worse part. In the past, after Eddie is born," seeing Bill's puzzled face, she added, "Your nephew. You two become grand friends."

Bill's eyes teared up, and Terrance reached over to hold his hand.

Connie took a deep breath and continued.

"Anyway, after Eddie was born, Theo had what he wanted. A son and the perfect wife. It was all the ideal cover for what he had been doing, and what he wanted to continue to do."

When Terrance moved to ask a question, Connie said, "Please, don't stop me. This is too hard to tell, and I have to say it all before I chicken out. No matter what you both think, this is true, all of it."

The two men nodded, hands clenched.

Taking a deep breath, Connie continued, "In the future, Theo beats Edith and Eddie. Edith dies. Eddie goes to live with your parents, but Theo wanted him back. As Theo drags Eddie from the house, Eddie hits his head on the concrete steps and dies."

"No! No! This didn't happen. My sister and nephew don't die that way. No. We would have stopped it!"

Connie wanted to rush over to Bill, hug him, and say that it never happened. But now that she had started, she had to finish.

"Yes, you would have, if you had known. But you know Edith, she would hide it. She wanted the perfect life. She went looking for it. She wouldn't have wanted to burden you with it. She let Theo do what he wanted to her, and she suspected to other women, because he promised never to touch Eddie.

"It's what those papers will prove to you. In the future, friends of mine go to your house. This house. They give you all the evidence I collected. You put it in your safe. That's what I hope shows up here."

"But even if all this is true, the information you collected is from the future, how could it show up here when it hasn't happened yet?"

"The same way that I am here. I died—a lonely woman—barely knowing my daughter. Never making friends because I was afraid that somehow they would discover my secret.

"And Eddie—yes, your nephew—found me in the in-between. A place where some people end up after they die.

"Sometimes they just have to realize that they are dead, and then they move on. Or, in some exceptional cases, they get a second chance to do what they should have done in their life.

"It was your sister that got me my chance. It's all about redemption, Bill. She got me a chance to redeem myself. She gave me a chance to make up for what I didn't do the first time."

"My sister?" Bill breathed out. "My sister dies, a nephew whom I don't even know yet, dies too, and then they help you after you die? How can this be true? You're right. It's hard not to think that you aren't crazy."

Terrance looked at Bill and then said, "But let's say that you are not. And that everything you have said is true. What happens now?"

Connie smiled at the two of them.

"Thank you for listening to me. It is crazy. It's hard to be this Connie and also the one that knows the future. Because I remember everything. I could tell you about the fantastic things that happen that would sound like magic. In a few months, a man will walk on the moon. But that's only the beginning. Technology changes everything.

"But it doesn't change the evil in people. It doesn't change the good either. And it's the good that I am following this time. Believe me, please. I know it seems impossible, but it's true.

"And I have a guide from the future who has been with me. I wish you could see him. He has been my lifeline, helping me be here in the past."

"Is that person here now?"

Connie looked over at Bryan, who had kept his promise to meet her here, and was standing beside Bill, and nodded yes.

It worried her that Bryan looked pale and exhausted. She hadn't thought about how draining all this must be for him.

"Yes. And he says that they put the papers into the safe. Please check again."

By then, neither Bill nor Terrance looked as if they believed her. It was as she had feared. They thought she was crazy. If the papers weren't in the safe, she would have to stop Theo on her own. That is, if she managed to get out of the room before they called someone to help her with her delusions.

As Bill twirled the lock on the safe, Terrance put his hand on Bill's shoulder and turned to Connie.

"Let's say all this is true. Wouldn't you not doing the same thing you did last time and then telling us all of this have changed things? What if they changed things for the worse?"

"Yes. Which makes all that I am doing even more terrifying. What if instead of making things better, I make it worse? But I couldn't be a coward again. I had to do something. And the only people I thought might believe me are the two of you."

Two things happened at the same time. Bill reached into the safe and pulled out a manila envelope that hadn't been there before, and a car screeched to a stop in front of the house.

The changes had begun.

FIFTY TWO

Eddie was in the middle of assisting an elderly woman into a boat when he felt it. Across the river, she could see all her friends and family waiting for her, but she couldn't cross alone. So it was up to Eddie to help her across to be with them.

Eddie knew there was no need for the boat or the river, but it was a scenario the woman had imagined for so long, it was what she saw. Which meant that no matter how strange he felt at the moment, he had to keep rowing.

Her story had to play out how she believed it. It wasn't up to him to change it, just to guide her out of the in-between where she had been stuck.

Besides, keeping his thought on her helped him forget what was going on with Connie.

He watched the woman's face grow brighter and brighter as she neared the shore. She stepped out of the boat with the help of her friends and was swallowed up in the crowd that welcomed her with hugs and laughter.

As soon as she was gone, so was the story, and Eddie found himself back in Bryan's living room, which surprised him. He had assumed that once Connie started changing what she had done in the past, he could no longer be part of Connie's journey.

But that wasn't the most surprising thing of all. It was who was there. Bryan was in his dad's lounge chair, looking as if he was asleep. Eddie knew that he wasn't. Bryan was probably off with Connie in a more physical form than usual. The woman he knew as Grace was in the kitchen doing something. He assumed that since Rachel wasn't there, Grace must have volunteered to make sure Bryan was okay.

But what delighted him, and terrified him, was that his mother and her friend Jillyan were there, too—smiling at him with her hand on Bryan's shoulder.

Eddie burst into tears, like the small boy that he was despite living all these years, and ran into his mother's arms. They hugged. He could feel her. It made him cry harder. She smoothed out his hair as she whispered, "Shh, it's okay. We'll be okay."

The grown man inside Eddie pulled back and looked up into Edith's eyes as he asked, "Are you sure? You're here because of what's going on in the past. You want to make sure you see me again, just in case, don't you?"

"Connie knows what she is doing. I trust that it will all work out. And you know as well as anyone that life doesn't end, it just moves on. We won't lose each other no matter what happens. On the other hand, we all ended up here together right now for a reason."

Just then, the doorbell rang, and Grace went to answer the door.

"Ava. What are you doing here?"

"I got the feeling that I was needed, so here I am."

As Ava walked into Bryan's living room, she stopped and said, "Oh. You have a few visitors."

"Visitors? It's just Bryan."

Ava laughed. "Nope. There are two women and a boy I assume is the boy Eddie that Rachel told us about."

"I'm confused," Eddie said, feeling as if he had lost the gist of the story.

Edith and Jillyan stood and said, "Welcome, Ava. We prompted you to come thinking Bryan might need some support in the past.

"I'm Edith, Eddie's mother, and this is Jillyan, Bryan's mother."

"I'm delighted to meet you. And honored."

"I'm guessing you are speaking to people I can't see, and not just to yourself?" Grace laughed. "I know I can't get them anything. But would you like coffee?"

Ava nodded yes and followed Grace into the kitchen to catch her up on who was in the living room. Edith followed them while Jillyan stayed with Bryan.

"Tell Grace that we can arrange it so she can see and hear us, if just for the time we are here, if she would like that."

Ava told Grace what Edith had said, and Grace had answered, "Yes, please." Carrying two cups of coffee, Grace returned to the living room and saw Eddie and the two women.

"Wow," was all she could say as she plopped into the nearest chair. Only years of experience kept her from spilling the coffee.

"Good. Now it will be easier for you to help," Edith said, "because Connie is in trouble."

* * * * * * * * * * *

In the meantime, in Pittsburgh, Bill said "Now what," after putting the documents in the safe.

Rachel looked over at Johnny, who shrugged his shoulders. "I guess now we wait."

"But for what?" Terrance asked. "Will we disappear? What will change? I guess I am back to asking questions I know nothing about. And even if things change, would we even know about it?"

At that moment, Johnny shot up and said, "Gotta go."

Remembering his manners, he turned back and shook both the men's hands.

"It's been a pleasure meeting you."

Seeing both their faces, he added, "I don't mean that I won't see you again. I just meant it the way it sounded. But Rachel and I need to get back to Doveland. I'm sure we will see each other again."

In the car, Rachel asked, "Are you sure?"

Johnny's glum face gave her the answer.

FIFTY THREE

"Pull over!" Johnny shouted. Until that moment, Rachel had thought he was sleeping, but when he started yelling to pull over, she realized he must have been somewhere else.

Rachel took the next exit and pulled into the McDonald's parking lot before asking, "What's going on?"

"Connie's in trouble. Bryan needs help. There is no time to get back to Bryan's house. I will have to help from here."

"Help how?"

"Dang. Too bad I can't call the police in the past to go to Bill's house right now."

Rachel watched as Johnny's face turned pale.

"Oh geez, this is bad."

"Are you there watching in the past?"

"Yes, along with Bryan and Ava. One of us will have to go back in the past to stop this."

Rachel just stared at Johnny, not understanding what she could do to help.

A moment later, Johnny added, "Okay, it will be me. Bryan has been keeping Connie calm, but doesn't have enough energy to pull this off."

Rachel shook her head, not understanding him at all, but willing to do whatever he needed.

"Just tell me what to do."

"Pull further away, back into that corner where the trees are. We don't want anyone to notice us. It might pull me back from the past."

Rachel backed up into the parking lot and then drove to the furthest end of the lot and parked under a stand of maple trees.

Johnny reached over and grabbed Rachel's hand. "Promise me you won't let go?"

As Rachel promised, Johnny's grip loosened, but hers remained firm. She knew exactly what to do.

· · · ● · ● · · ·

Theo didn't bother ringing the doorbell or knocking on the door, and although Connie had run to the front door to lock it, she was too late. Theo slammed his way into the foyer and pushed Connie up against the wall, his hand on her throat.

"I thought I told you to get lost, you little bitch," he hissed into her face.

As Bill and Terrance came around the corner, Theo turned to them and said, "Don't come nearer, you fags. Did you think I didn't know? I always know. Shocked? You shouldn't be. Now, if you move, I'll push so hard that I'll crush her windpipe."

The two men held up their hands and took one step back.

Theo reached around Connie and pulled her arm behind her back, twisting her, so she was facing away from him and, keeping his other arm across her neck, started pushing her towards the room he had seen Bill and Terrance come from.

"Go," he said to Bill and Terrance. "Go, or I break her arm."

Once they got to the study, he directed the two men to sit on the chairs stationed in front of Bill's desk, pushing Connie into the desk chair. When the men didn't move, he reached behind his back and pulled out a gun.

"Sit!"

Addressing Bill, he added, "Throw me your necktie. Might as well do something with that little fairy piece of cloth."

Bill took off his necktie and tossed in on the desk.

"No, bring it here and tie this bitch's hands behind her back."

When Bill didn't move, Theo waved the gun at him.

"Move. It would be easier to shoot her than tie her up. So if you care about her, do what I said. Then use your belt to tie up your boyfriend there, too."

Once he had tied Connie and Terrance's hands behind their backs, Bill returned to his chair. Theo stepped back, keeping the gun pointed at the three of them, but looking at Connie.

"I suppose you told them what happened? Now I have to decide what to do about the three of you, not just you. So if something happens to them, it will be your fault. I told you to keep quiet, or I would hurt someone, but no, you didn't listen. I didn't think you would. It's why I had you followed.

"You have been a pain in my ass from the beginning. Edith is the perfect wife for me, as long as you are not her friend. Now, you have caused your own death and your friends' because I will not let you ruin my perfect life.

"You think I don't have a plan? I do. I always have a plan."

Outside the window, Connie could see the branches of the dogwood tree glowing green as the sun shone behind them. A squirrel ran across the branch, causing a shower of rain to drop off, glinting gold. It was beautiful. So simple. Not confusing.

Just a tree, a squirrel, the sun, and drops of water.

Why did people have to make life so complicated?

Looking up at Theo, she said, "There is no way to get rid of us, Theo. If you kill the three of us, people will notice. They will figure out it's you. You might as well run."

"I can't run, and you know it. My parents control my life, my money, my future. I need them. I need Edith. I don't need you."

Theo's gaze traveled to where the safe lay open.

"What were you getting out of the safe, Bill?"

Seeing a manila envelope on the desk, he handed it to Bill.

"Open it, show me what's inside."

Bill's hand shook as he took out the papers and put them on the desk.

Theo picked up a photocopy of a newspaper clipping. A picture of a missing girl stared out at him. Connie knew he recognized the girl. His face turned pale and then red. He rummaged through the rest of the papers. Some of them had his name on them.

"What is this? What the hell is going on?"

Shoving the gun into Connie's face, he said, "Tell me, or I will shoot you one body part at a time."

Connie shrugged, what could she lose?

"I'm not the Connie you raped a few days ago, you ass-hole. I am from the future, come back to stop you."

Theo stared at her and then pulled back and laughed. "You think that story will distract me? How stupid can you be, trying to pretend that you are crazy, and from the future?

"Yea, right! Does your future self know how I will kill the three of you?"

"Well, if I am not from the future, how do I know that there is someone at the door right now?"

Theo paused. The doorbell rang, and he laughed.

"Good guess. Okay, Bill, get rid of this person, or else they will join the three of you, and you will be responsible for their death.

I know—goody two shoes that you are—that will kill you. Ha. As if you won't be dead, anyway."

After Theo pushed Bill to the front door, the gun digging into Bill's back, Connie smiled and whispered to the young man standing behind Terrance and asked, "Can you do it?"

Looking into Terrance's terrified face, she added, "Shh, don't be afraid. A friend is here, and he has called the police."

Moments later, as he pushed Bill into the room, Theo shouted, "There was no one there."

Too late, he noticed that neither Terrance nor Connie were in their chairs.

FIFTY FOUR

"**I**'ll shoot him if you don't come back!" Theo yelled.

No one answered him.

"I'll shoot you anyway, you scumbag," Theo whispered in Bill's ear.

Bill was just as confused as Theo about where Connie and Terrance had gone, but he was grateful they had gotten away.

"It seems to me that you have two choices. Shoot me and run. Or just run. At the moment, no one but us knows what you have done.

"And the papers you saw? Who will believe them? They talk about things that haven't happened yet. You know the police. They need concrete evidence. Those papers won't work."

Theo poked Bill in the ribs. "Sure. But you three are talkers. I already told Connie not to talk, and then here she is blabbing her mouth off."

"Let's say we do. Who will they believe, you or us?"

As Theo thought about what Bill said, two things happened at the same time. His grip loosened slightly on the gun, and something pushed him to the side.

Then that something pushed him harder, knocking the gun from his hand, and it went flying across the room. Both Theo and Bill stared at the gun lying on the floor, stunned at what had happened. Theo reacted first. He started towards the gun, but then, hearing police sirens, turned, and ran towards the door.

But Terrance was already there. This time he grabbed Theo's arm and twisted it around his back and walked him back into the office. Bill had kicked the gun further away, and Connie was standing beside him.

"Bill was right, you know, Theo. You might be able to convince the police you did nothing wrong. But, you see, I have evidence that you did. I know how to find those girls, I know how to point the authorities towards what they need to know to put you in prison.

"You know how I know this, Theo? Because I am from the future. In the past, I made a mistake. I didn't tell anyone. I let you live out your life destroying others. I never told Edith or tried to save her."

Connie grabbed a clipping off the desk.

"Look. See. She dies. But she spends nine long years with you, first with you betraying her, and then punishing her for anything you didn't like about her. You beat her, Theo, and I never stepped in to stop you.

"I was a coward. I killed her, too, because I didn't speak out. Well, not this time."

Theo spit.

"I knew you were a bitch. I don't care what you say. You aren't from the future. I don't know what kind of trick this is, but you won't get away with it. I'll destroy you and your queer friends here."

Connie laughed.

"Ah, so I haven't convinced you yet. Let me give it another try. I have a few friends here from the future. You can't see them. Sorry, but I can. If you could see them, you might think they are ghosts. And usually, spirits, ghosts, people from the future, can't deal with physical objects. However, in the future, when you learn about quantum physics, you find that sometimes they can."

Theo giggled hysterically.

"Yea, right? Spirits, ghosts, people from the future. Just keep talking like that, and you'll end up in the loony bin."

Looking at Bill, he asked, "You don't actually believe this crap, do you?"

"Afraid that I do," Bill said. "Otherwise, who untied their hands? Who knocked the gun out of your hand?"

Connie laughed again.

"That was Johnny. You'll never meet him, Theo. But another man named Bryan is here too.

He's the son of Edith's friend, Jillyan. Oh, you probably never met her because Edith had to hide her friendships from you.

"Perhaps they could give you a little demonstration?"

Theo snorted, but when something slapped him across the face, and when the window flew open, he turned pale.

"I don't know how you did that, but it's a trick."

"Okay. One last trick, then. Perhaps you would like to meet your son, Eddie? Eddie, the son, whose death you also caused. By mistake, it turns out, but still, he died."

"No. Not true."

"True, father," Eddie said.

FIFTY FIVE

Back in Bryan's living room, the women held hands. Edith had told them what they needed to do, and they were doing it without question.

Grace was grateful that she could see Eddie, Jillyan, and Edith because it made it easier to send all her energy their way.

Ava was directing what they all needed to do. Ava kept herself in the present while monitoring what was happening in the past.

When Johnny and Bryan didn't convince Theo, Ava was the one that explained to Eddie what he needed to do.

At first, he had said, "Absolutely not."

But Edith confirmed what Ava said. It was the only way. He had to confront Theo, or all that they had been doing would fail.

Things would change, but if they didn't stop Theo, they would not be for the better.

Finally, Eddie bowed his head and said, "Okay, I'll go."

A moment later, Bryan woke to find his mother standing by his side.

In the car in the McDonald's parking lot, Johnny woke to find Rachel holding his hand.

Grace watched as the scene in the living room shifted, and then she was alone with Bryan and Ava.

"Are they gone?" she whispered.

When Ava nodded, Bryan burst into tears.

FIFTY SIX

By the time the police arrived, having received an anonymous call, Theo was no longer a threat.

The police, having known Theo for years and having arrested him time and time again and never been able to charge him with anything, stoically did their duty, thinking that it wouldn't matter, anyway. But in the past, Theo would threaten and charm, resisting. This time, he seemed frozen in place.

Right before the police entered the office, the scattered papers from the future vanished from the desktop, and Theo had started to shake.

"You," he said, looking at Connie, hatred dripping from his voice.

Turning to the two officers, he said, "That bitch is from the future. She came back to destroy my life."

One officer shook his head and looked at Connie, Bill, and Terrance standing quietly by the window. The other two officers exchanged looks behind Theo's back.

It was easy to see what they were thinking. The guy had gone crazy.

Bill pointed out where the gun had slid across the floor.

That made all three officers smile. A gun. This time they might be able to keep him in jail after all.

One officer stayed behind to take their statement.

Bill and Theo let Connie do the talking. She explained that Theo had raped her a few days earlier and threatened to permanently shut her up if she talked.

It had taken her a few days to get the courage to speak to Bill. She hadn't wanted to tell her best friend, Edith, about her husband. She still didn't, even though she knew it had to be done.

Theo had found out that she had gone to Bill's house and figured it was because she wanted to tell Bill and Terrance what happened.

"So, he threatened you with a gun?" The officer asked.

"He did," Connie answered.

"Well, let's hope his parents don't bail him out of this one, but a gun and three witnesses should make our case this time. But how did the gun end up on the floor?"

Connie explained that although she and Terrance were tied up, Bill wasn't. Then the doorbell rang, and Theo and Bill had gone to see who was there. While they were gone, Terrance had managed to untie his hands—Bill hadn't tied them very tight—and she and Terrance had slipped out of the room.

When Theo saw that they were missing, he was so shocked that his grip on the gun loosened, and Bill was able to push him, so the gun slid away. Then Terrance came in, and the two of them subdued Theo.

"Okay," the officer said, "But who was at the door? And who called the police?"

"I guess we were lucky," Bill said. "It must have been a prank. No one was at the door."

"And Terrance called the police when we left the room," Connie added. "But then came back quickly to help Bill."

"Well, I think that will do it. Do you have any reason why he thinks you are from the future?"

Connie smiled. "No idea, officer. But I am pressing charges. Maybe Theo wants to make people think I'm crazy."

"Probably," the officer said. Tipping his hat, he added, "We'll need you later, but in the meantime perhaps you should talk to his wife, since she is your friend, before we do. It might be better that way."

"We'll go with you, Connie," Bill said, and Terrance nodded. "And I am calling my parents to meet us there too. I think we all need to face this together."

On the way over, Connie hid her terror the best that she could. She had been calm during the police interview, but that calmness was hiding her fear.

She had done what she needed to do. Now what would happen? What would Edith say? Would she hate her forever for bringing this horror to her door?

Plus, what had happened to the future now that she had put all these changes in place? What would happen to her? Would she forget that she was from the future, or would she live out the rest of the life here now, with this new reality? Connie knew that Bill and Terrance were asking themselves the same questions. But it was too late now to worry about that part.

From now on, it had to be about Edith and Eddie, and the baby she already knew would be a girl, and she would call her Karla.

What would happen after that, she didn't know, but what she did know was that she would meet everything life had for her by facing it and not running away.

Bill and Terrance smiled at her in the rearview mirror, and she smiled back. She had a feeling that it would be a wonderful life, after all.

EPILOGUE

Connie was tired. It had been a wonderful life. Much better, the second time around.

Karla poked her head in the room and saw her son Edward reading his favorite book, Charlotte's Web, to his grandmother.

Her mother was beaming at him, even though Karla could tell that she was so tired she just wanted to sleep. But Connie had said she would not waste a single moment with her grandson.

Her uncles Bill and Terrance were on their way. They said they would hire a driver, and not to worry about them. Nothing would keep them away. Connie had asked to see them, and that meant they were coming no matter what.

Karla ducked her head out of the room before her mother saw her crying. Besides, she had a small army of people she would have to feed. She couldn't remember a time when her mother wasn't helping everyone, and now they all wanted to say thank you.

Connie said that when she died—well not died, but moved to another place—she wouldn't be able to talk to her friends and tell them how much they meant to her. She had to do it now.

It was funny, Karla thought. Mom always talked about these things as if she knew something about them. But how could she?

"Karla, we're here. Where do you want all this stuff?"

Karla laughed as she helped her half-brother, Eddie, and her husband, unload all the supplies onto her mother's kitchen table.

She had never heard the entire story of how she and Eddie ended up having the same father, but their mothers had loved them both as if they were each their own.

When they were older, Karla and Eddie had visited Theo, but their father's mind had been lost years before he died and he didn't know either of them.

Eddie had comforted her and said it was better that way, and she believed him. He was always so much wiser than her.

Sometimes she would catch Eddie daydreaming, and he would tell her that it was nothing, but she knew it wasn't. It felt to her that in those moments he had been somewhere else.

Eddie's mother Edith had passed away a few years before, and Connie had faded after that. She had caught Eddie and her mother quietly talking together more than once, as if they had a secret they shared.

When she had mentioned to her mother that she felt as if Edith was still around watching over her, Connie had smiled and answered, "I'm sure she is."

Karla wasn't sure if she was humoring her or if she was serious.

"Do you need help with anything?"

Coming back to the present, she went to hug the two people who had just arrived, Bryan and Rachel. Mom's friends from forever, although she had never heard the story of how they met.

Bryan and Rachel had known each other from childhood. But it had taken them a while to get together.

"Better late than never," Rachel had told her one day.

"Grandma says she wants to talk to you," Edward said as he entered the kitchen.

"Who, honey?"

"She says Uncle Eddie will know."

Karla looked at Eddie and realized that he did know. It was why Bryan and Rachel were here. They were part of that secret, too. None of them would tell her what it was, so she had given up asking.

Taking Edward's hand, she said, "Come help me pick some flowers from the garden for your grandmother's room."

· · · ● · ● · ● · ● · · ●

The three of them found Connie, awake and smiling.

"I just wanted to thank the three of you for helping me to redeem myself. There is no way I could ever repay you myself, but I think that life has done that for each of you. I know that it has for me.

"Eddie, me being able to be your mother too, along with Edith, well, that is a gift that is so priceless I have no words. And then to have a grandson. It's more than I ever dreamed would happen.

"And Rachel and Bryan. You two were, and are, angels. Thank you."

When the three of them looked worried, she added, "No, I am not leaving just yet. I asked to see all these people so I could say a proper goodbye to them.

"After that, though, you know I have some other friends waiting for me. I know you see your mother all the time, Eddie, but I am afraid that she is waiting for me. We have places to go together."

Eddie leaned down and hugged Connie. "You two have fun! And thank you for being brave and making all of our lives better. It's because of you that I had an entire lifetime with mom."

As the three of them turned to leave the room, Connie called after them.

"Eddie, if you have a direct line to whoever made sure we remembered it all, will you tell them 'Thank you?'"

Eddie smiled as he said, "Connie, you can thank her yourself. And tell my mom thank you from me, too.

"Although there are times I thought it would be easier not to know, I also wouldn't have wanted it any other way."

Rachel and Bryan nodded in agreement, closed the door softly behind them, and smiled at each other.

Thanks to Connie, Eddie, Edith, and Jillyan, they had a wedding to plan.

This book was inspired by something I read when I was eighteen. It only took me over fifty years to write about it.

In my first year of college at Penn State, I had a French class that I adored. Very unusual for me since French in high school inspired fear in my heart.

Why did I love that class? Two reasons: an exceptional teacher and because we read a book that made a deep impression on me. Throughout the years, I would often think of the essence of that story.

I remembered that two people met in the afterlife, who should have met when they were alive. So they were given a chance to return to life and see if they could fix that mistake.

Life continuing, connections, redemption—who doesn't want all that?

When I started writing this book, I went looking for the original book. I had looked before but had had no luck finding it.

Then one day, in the middle of writing this book, I saw the phrase, "the die is cast" in an article about political incompetence, and tried once more. This time, I was successful.

Although I remember our French teacher translating the title as The Die Is Cast, I now see it translated as The Chips Are Down.

If you can read French (I can't anymore), you can read Jean-Paul Satre's book, Les Jeux Sont Fait. It's also a movie made in 1947.

If not, I hope you like my humble rendition of the theme that life continues, connections both here and There, and perhaps it is possible to return to life and redeem ourselves. —Beca

PS

Thank you for reading my books. Otherwise, it would just be

me and the words, and although words are lovely, it's the sharing of them that makes it all worthwhile. Thank you for reading and sharing mine.

You can find all of my books at your favorite book store or on my website: becalewis.com

· · · ● ● · ● · ● · ● · · ·

CONNECT WITH ME ONLINE:

Facebook: https://www.facebook.com/becalewiscreative
Facebook: https://www.facebook.com/becalewisfans
Instagram: https://instagram.com/becalewis
TikTok: https://tiktok.com/@becalewis
Twitter: http://twitter.com/becalewis
LinkedIn: https://linkedin.com/in/becalewis
Youtube: https://www.youtube.com/c/becalewis

Acknowledgements

I could never write a book without the help of my friends and my book community. Thank you, Jet Tucker, Jamie Lewis, Diana Cormier, and Barbara Budan for taking the time to do the final reader proof. You are a loyal and much-loved reader team. You can't imagine how much I appreciate it.

A huge thank you to Laura Moliter for her fantastic book editing.

Thank you to every other member of my Book Community who helps me make so many decisions that help the book be the best book possible.

Thank you to all the people who tell me that they love to read these stories. Those random comments from friends and strangers are more valuable than gold.

And as always, thank you to my beloved husband, Del, for being my daily sounding board, for putting up with all my questions, my constant need to want to make things better, and for being the love of my life, in more than just this one lifetime.

Also By Beca

The Rivers of Time Series: Women's Lit, Friendship, Small Town, Mystery, Magical Realism, Small Town Fiction
The Returning, The Awakening, The Rising

Follow Me Here: **Women's Lit, Friendship, Small Town, Mystery, Magical Realism, Small Town Fiction**

The Ruby Sisters Series: Women's Lit, Friendship, Mystery, Small Town Fiction
A Last Gift, After All This Time, And Then She Remembered, As If It Was Real, Almost Innocent

Stories From Doveland: Women's Lit, Friendship, Small Town, Mystery, Magical Realism, Small Town Fiction
Karass, Pragma, Jatismar, Exousia, Stemma, Paragnosis, In-Between, Missing, Out Of Nowhere

The Return To Erda Series: Fantasy
Shatterskin, Deadsweep, Abbadon, The Experiment

The Chronicles of Thamon: Fantasy
Banished, Betrayed, Discovered, Wren's Story

The Shift Series: Spiritual Self-Help
Living in Grace: The Shift to Spiritual Perception
The Daily Shift: Daily Lessons From Love To Money
The 4 Essential Questions: Choosing Spiritually Healthy Habits
The 28 Day Shift To Wealth: A Daily Prosperity Plan
The Intent Course: Say Yes To What Moves You
Imagination Mastery: A Workbook For Shifting Your Reality
Right Thinking: A Thoughtful System for Healing
Perception Mastery: Seven Steps To Lasting Change
Blooming Your Life: How To Experience Consistent Happiness

Perception Parables: Very short stories
Love's Silent Sweet Secret: A Fable About Love
Golden Chains And Silver Cords: A Fable About Letting Go

Advice / Journals
A Woman's ABC's of Life: Lessons in Love, Life, and Career from
Those Who Learned The Hard Way
The Daily Nudge(s): So When Did You First Notice

OTHER PLACES TO FIND BECA

- Facebook: facebook.com/becalewiscreative

- Instagram: instagram.com/becalewis

- LinkedIn: linkedin.com/in/becalewis

- Youtube: www.youtube.com/c/becalewis

- Buy Books Direct: https://becalewis.org/

About Beca

Beca writes books she hopes will change people's perceptions of themselves and the world, and open possibilities to things and ideas that are waiting to be seen and experienced.

At sixteen, Beca founded her own dance studio. Later, she received a Master's Degree in Dance in Choreography from UCLA and founded the Harbinger Dance Theatre, a multimedia dance company, while continuing to run her dance school.

After graduating—to better support her three children—Beca switched to the sales field, where she worked as an employee and independent contractor in many industries, excelling in each while perfecting and teaching her Shift System and writing books.

She joined the financial industry in 1983 and became an Associate Vice President of Investments at a major stock brokerage firm. She was a licensed Certified Financial Planner for over twenty years.

This diversity, along with a variety of life challenges, helped fuel the desire to share what she's learned by writing and speaking, hoping it will make a difference in other people's lives.

Beca grew up in State College, PA, with the dream of becoming a dancer and then a writer. She carried that dream forward as she fulfilled a childhood wish by moving to Southern California in 1968. Beca told her family she would never move back to the cold.

After living there for thirty-one years, she met her husband, Delbert Lee Piper, Sr., at a retreat in Virginia, and everything changed. They decided to find a place they could call their own, which sent them off traveling around the United States. They lived and worked in a few different places before returning to live in the cold once again near Del's family in a small town in Northeast Ohio, not too far from State College.

When not working and teaching together, they love to visit and play with their combined family of eight children and five grandchildren, walk, read, study, do yoga or taiji, feed birds, and work in their garden.